# HUMAN

# SOLUTIONS

# HUMAN

# SOLUTIONS

## AVI SILBERSTEIN

Skyhorse Publishing

Skyhorse Publishing books may be purchased in bulk at special discounts for sales promotion, corporate gifts, fund-raising, or educational purposes. Special editions can also be created to specifications. For details, contact the Special Sales Department, Skyhorse Publishing, 307 West 36th Street, 11th Floor, New York, NY 10018 or info@skyhorsepublishing.com.

Skyhorse® and Skyhorse Publishing® are registered trademarks of Skyhorse Publishing, Inc.®, a Delaware corporation.

Visit our website at www.skyhorsepublishing.com.

10 9 8 7 6 5 4 3 2 1

Library of Congress Cataloging-in-Publication Data is available on file.

ISBN: 978-1-62873-714-1

Printed in the United States of America

# HUMAN

# SOLUTIONS

# ONE

A young woman walked into the office and asked to see me.

"Make her wait half an hour," I said to my secretary.

She returned to the reception to tell the woman I was busy and would see her shortly. I worked on another file until my secretary poked her head in again.

"How about now?" she said.

I nodded without looking up from my work. The woman entered the room, and my secretary quietly shut the door behind her.

"I don't want to know your name," I said as she was sitting down.

The woman leaned forward and looked at me attentively.

"Okay," she said.

"So?"

"I'm in love with the weatherman," said the woman.

"Your name is Laura."

"I have an Aunt Laura," she said. "Could we change it to something else?"

I pulled out a pad of yellow legal paper and told her to start talking.

Laura was twenty-eight years old. She had been in a couple of long-term relationships and in several short ones. She was—by her own admission—attractive, intelligent and funny. She did not have any trouble meeting men. Every night she watched the news on television, just so she could see the weatherman.

"You don't understand," she said. She was right—I didn't. "But every time they say 'over to you, Diego, for a look at the weather,' my heart starts to go."

I pretended to be taking notes.

"His energy," Laura said, "is the most powerful force I have ever encountered. It just about blows me off my feet."

I had seen the weatherman on television. His name was Diego. He was a young man, probably in his early thirties, adequately handsome, and overly enthusiastic about his often erroneous predictions.

"I see," I said.

"I don't want you to think I'm crazy," Laura said. "I'm not a stalker, and I'm not obsessed. I just think it would be fun to get to meet him sometime and see if we hit it off."

I nodded.

"I don't want to be inappropriate," Laura said, "but there are certain things that he says that make my knees melt. When he talks about 'humid conditions'—just the way he says that word. Humid. What his lips do when he says that word."

I frowned and concerned myself with appearing to write.

"Or when there's a natural disaster warning," she continued. "A mud slide or something like that, the way his eyebrows move towards each other when he's looking concerned."

I shifted in my seat and cleared my throat. Then I told Laura that we would take her on as a client. She clapped her hands together and thanked me.

"How did you find out about us?" I said.

Laura looked uncomfortable. "I was telling a friend of mine about Diego, and she told me about you."

"Which friend?" I said.

"Oh, I shouldn't say."

I raised my eyebrows at her. "Yes, you should."

Laura rotated one of her earrings.

"Gabriela," she said, finally, "Gabriela Morales."

I noted this on my pad of paper. Gabriela would be receiving a referral invoice from us shortly. She would be expecting it.

"What did Gabriela tell you?" I said.

"She didn't say much. Just that you helped her get her in-laws to stop hating her."

"Here's what I can tell you," I said. "We are called Human Solutions, but you won't find that anywhere. Not in the phone book, not in any directory or business bureau. As far as anyone is concerned, we don't exist."

Laura nodded eagerly.

"We are in the business of making things happen," I said. "If you want the weatherman to fall in love with you, we'll make it happen. If there's a job that you really want, we'll make it happen. If you're lonely and want more friends, we'll make it happen. Anything."

"But how?"

"Our job is to worry about the how. Your job is to give us all the information we need and to do exactly what we say."

Laura considered this. "What about payment?"

I explained about our fee structure—there would be an initial lump sum and then subsequent payments depending on the length of time required to complete the Manipulation.

"This is the initial lump sum," I said. I wrote a number down on a piece of paper and handed it to her.

Laura looked at it and shrugged.

"How are you going to afford that?"

She told me her last name. It was the name of Chile's major grocery chain.

"One more thing," I said, "about payment. We will also need a written guarantee that you will help us with future Manipulations—on our side, we guarantee that our requests will be acceptable and not unreasonable."

"All right," Laura said. "I'll do it."

She stuck her hand out across the table. I shook it—her skin was soft, but her grip was firm.

"What if it doesn't work?" Laura said.

"The Manipulation?"

"Yes."

"It always works."

"Always?"

I gestured towards the door. "If you don't mind," I said.

# TWO

After Laura had left, I walked out to the reception area. It was a vacant space—a desk, a couple of chairs, nothing more. I asked my secretary to schedule a meeting with Julio and Rodolfo for sometime that afternoon.

"Tell them we've got a new client," I said.

She wrote herself a note.

"I'm going out for lunch," I said.

"And when will you be back?"

This was a new secretary—I ignored her question and walked out into the bustle of downtown Santiago. The lunch crowd was spilling from tall buildings and filing neatly into cafes and restaurants and sandwich shops. I went to my usual place—German Lunch Pail, it was called. I sat at the bar and waited until my waitress came by with a glass of water. "The usual, Javier?" she said.

"With salad this time. No fries."

"Come on—no fries?"

"Some fries. Two or three fries, but some salad too."

"Okay, okay," she said, rubbing my shoulder.

Maybe I would come here for lunch with my secretary. Just for learning's sake.

The waitress came by with a glass of dark beer and the newspaper.

"Are you still married?" I said.

"Same as yesterday," she said. "Ask me again tomorrow."

I took a sip of the beer. When my food arrived, I rotated the plate until it was lined up right—French fries on the left, salad at the top, and sandwich on the right. The sandwich was a delicious mess of thinly-sliced pieces of steak, melted cheese, fried onion, tomato, avocado, and mayonnaise. There was nothing German about this place other than some imported beer and the best apple *küchen* in the city.

I didn't very much like eating alone, but it seemed to be happening more and more. I reached for the newspaper, *El Mercurio*, and flapped the pages around until I got it to fold right. The newspaper was not much more than a placeholder these days. The Dictator—General Pinochet—had an iron grip on the media. There had not been much dissent in the mainstream media in the fifteen years since the day he had taken over the country—September 11, 1973—but, somewhere beneath the thin layers of black print, there was an audible grumbling coming from both left and right. Tensions were running high in this country.

"Some dessert?" said the waitress.

"I have a meeting this afternoon," I said. "I need to be a little bit hungry sometimes if I want to get things done."

I looked up. She was still standing there, but, somewhere inside, she was already at the next table, collecting her tip, then clocking out, then at home, taking off the ridiculous German-barmaid outfit they made her wear.

# THREE

I had my secretary boil some water for instant coffee.

"I could go buy some cookies," she said.

Julio shook his head. "No, no, don't bother." Julio had once been a professor of Sociology at the *Universidad Católica de Chile*. Immediately following Pinochet's takeover, he was removed from his position after refusing to withdraw from the lectures any mention of the upsides of Communism and Socialism. He had gone back to school and become a psychotherapist. I asked after his wife and kids; he asked after my students at the Acting Studio.

Rodolfo burst in, with half a sandwich dangling from his hands. He scratched his beard and settled comfortably into a chair. He worked three days a week as a private investigator and two days a week for Human Solutions.

We exchanged pleasantries, and then I cleared my throat. I shuffled through the papers on my desk until I found my notes. Then I recounted my meeting with Laura that morning. Julio took off his glasses and closed his eyes as I stood and spoke. Rodolfo tracked my pacing and gesturing, only occasionally making direct eye contact.

When I was done, we came up with a list of questions that we needed to have answered—who were Diego's friends, what did he do in his spare time, what was his living situation, etc. Nothing could be done until we knew more.

"I'll do some surveillance," Rodolfo said.

"We'll meet in a few days," I said.

By the time Julio and Rodolfo left, it was dark outside. I tried to finish up some paperwork but couldn't get anything done. My secretary came in to tell me she was going home.

"I'll walk you to the subway," I said. "I'm going there myself."

She looked embarrassed. "I have a date," she said. "We're meeting at a restaurant right near here."

I looked back down at my papers. "Have fun," I said, without looking up. "I'll see you Wednesday."

The phone was just sitting there, so I called up my sister.

"You sound like a woman who wants to go for a drink," I said when she picked up.

"Only my brother could know me that well," she said. "But we're going to a party at our friends' house."

I grunted and tapped my fingers on the desk.

"Hey, Javier," she said. "Why don't you come with us?"

"I need to get back to work. We'll go for that drink some other time."

"You're thirty-eight years old, and you're single," she said. "You're coming to this party whether you like it or not."

"I have a prior commitment."

"We'll pick you up in twenty minutes."

She hung up. I carefully put the phone down on the receiver. Then I slid open my desk drawer and lifted out a clean shirt.

# FOUR

María Paz and her husband picked me up in their sedan.

"What's this dinner party?" I said.

"Just some friends," María Paz said. "That shirt looks nice on you."

"I picked it up some time ago. I don't wear it much."

She looked at me in the rearview mirror. "I bought it for your birthday two years ago," she said.

It seemed unlikely but not impossible. I changed the subject by asking María Paz's husband about his job—he was a civil engineer. Then I let the conversation peter out, and we rode the rest of the way in silence.

The party was in a rural section of the city, partway up one of the mountains that encircle Santiago. The view was something else—all broad mountains and winding canyons. I fished a bottle of beer out of a washtub filled with ice and looked around to see if I knew anyone. María Paz and her husband had vanished, and I had that awful feeling you get when you're standing alone at a party. It was the same blend of exclusion and loneliness that I get at an airport when my fellow passengers are greeted with hugs and kisses at the arrivals area, and I am left looking for signage to the taxis.

I saw a group of men standing around a large hole in the ground. I went up to get a closer look.

"What's this all about?" I said to the man next to me.

"*Curanto en hoyo*," he said. "They eat it in the South. We made a fire in the hole this morning and heated up a bunch of rocks. Then we wrapped big leaves around fish and oysters and clams and potatoes and carrots, and covered it all in dirt. Now we're digging it up."

I stared down at the food that was being carefully pulled from the dirt. The man introduced himself. He began to tell me about a childhood memory of eating *curanto en hoyo*, so I roped a bystander into our conversation and then quietly escaped.

There were a number of bottles of red wine on a table. I helped myself to a glass. My sister caught my eye and waved me over to where she was talking to a woman. I pretended not to notice, until she called out for me to come meet her friend. After downing the glass, I refilled it and walked over to where they stood.

"I," said the woman, "am just *so* impressed by the things María Paz has been telling me."

I looked at my sister with a blank face. She smiled.

"Now what's with this acting studio your sister mentioned?"

"Sorry, I'm being rude," María Paz said. "Javier, this is Elena—Oh! There's Soledad!"

María Paz hurried away, and I took a long sip of my wine.

"You were going to say," Elena said. "About the acting studio?"

"I run an acting studio. I teach people how to act."

"I always wanted to act! You've been doing it for a while?"

I told her a little more and asked what she did to keep busy. She was a colour psychologist—someone who conducts studies to examine the feelings evoked by showing people different colours.

"For instance, if a cereal company wants to launch a new cereal, they would hire me to determine what colour combinations to use for the box—a process involving numerous surveys and dozens of cereal-box iterations being shown to hundreds of subjects. I'm then able to advise the company on which colour combinations induced hunger, or excitement, or pleasure, or low self-esteem, or whatever they want."

It was an interesting concept, and I wanted to know more—the possible uses in future Manipulations came to mind—but Elena had begun touching my arm every so often, and I was ready to get away. I'm suspicious of women who seem to like me before they know the first thing about me.

"It's been a pleasure," I said and gestured towards my empty wine glass, "but I must go find the washroom."

I went into the house but was not particularly in need of a washroom. I wandered into the kitchen and found some crackers and cheese. A man walked into the room and rummaged around in the cupboards until he found a glass. He walked over to the sink and filled it with water and then turned to me.

"That woman you were talking to," he said, "is something else."

I ate a cracker and nodded noncommittally.

"May I ask, is she your wife?"

"She's not," I said.

"Is she your girlfriend, then?"

It occurred to me that there was nothing at all wrong with Elena—she was good-looking and interesting and bright.

"She's not my girlfriend," I said, "but I'm just in the process of asking her to dinner."

"Well, if she's not your girlfriend—"

I held up a hand to interrupt him. "Tell you what," I said. "If she says, 'No,' I'll make sure to come over and let you know, so that you can try your luck."

I left the room before he could give this proper consideration. I hurried outside and found Elena in the middle of a spirited conversation with an older man.

"Sorry to interrupt," I said to the older man. I pulled Elena aside by her elbow and placed one of my business cards in her hand.

"I'd like to take you out to dinner," I said. "Perhaps sometime this weekend?"

Elena smiled. "That would be lovely."

"Great," I said. "Give me a call, and we'll figure out the details."

I walked her back over to the old man and left them both to continue their conversation. The prospect of having dinner with someone who actually seemed like an interesting person was simultaneously exciting and frightening. I wanted the company, the partnership—but as much as we try, we can never have full control over how other people behave or what might happen to them.

María Paz was nowhere to be found, but her husband materialized by my side. I told him about Elena, and he slapped my shoulder. We went to look for María Paz and found her sitting at a table with a large plate of oysters.

"You look like you need some help eating those," I said. She nodded vigorously—like someone who has consumed too much wine. The three of us ate the oysters and then another plateful.

# FIVE

Rodolfo stirred some milk into his coffee. He added three lumps of sugar and looked over at me.

"Shall I begin?" he said.

I nodded. Julio took out a pad of paper and settled back into his chair.

"Here are some photos of Diego," Rodolfo said, handing us a small stack of black-and-white surveillance photos. Diego walking out of his apartment. Diego on the phone at his window. Diego playing soccer in the park.

Rodolfo brushed cookie crumbs off his shirt and continued. Diego lived in an old apartment building in a gentrifying neighborhood. He spent most of his free time playing soccer with friends and drinking beer at a bar near his place. Rodolfo briefed us on when Diego usually went to bed and when he awoke. He told us what he bought at the grocery store and what books he checked out from the library.

"Here's what I think," Julio said. "Let's give him a new friend, and then we'll set up a big meeting. Group encounters seem to work best with young people."

I nodded and made a note on my legal pad. We discussed the logistics of giving Diego a new friend. I would have to pick one of my actors to play the role.

Just as Julio and Rodolfo were gathering their papers, the phone rang, and my secretary picked up. She buzzed me, and I picked up the phone.

"Sorry to disturb," she said. "It's a woman on the phone for you—Elena."

I covered the receiver and looked over at Julio and Rodolfo. "I should take this," I said, nodding towards the door. I waited until Julio and Rodolfo left the office. I took a deep breath and got back on the phone. "You can put the call through. My meeting is done."

There was a click and then her voice. "Javier?"

"Yes, speaking. Who is this?"

"It's Elena."

"Elena, Elena . . ."

"We met at the barbecue earlier this week."

"Of course, yes."

"You mentioned at the party that maybe you wanted to have dinner this weekend?"

"Oh, this weekend is awfully busy," I said. "But maybe a late dinner on Saturday would work for me. And for you?"

"Well yes—"

"Great—I'll put you through to my secretary and have her take down your address. I'm in a meeting right now."

I wished her a good day and put the call back through to my secretary. I got up and went to put on my jacket. I needed a walk and maybe a drink. My secretary looked up at me and gave a little wave as I walked through the reception area. It was unseasonally cold outside, but I didn't mind much.

# SIX

The next day, I was at the Acting Studio. The studio was a large vacant warehouse in an industrial part of Santiago. I had twenty or so students, almost equal parts women and men. The youngest was 15 years old, and the oldest was 72. That was good—we needed a wide range for most Manipulations.

The deal was simple: I gave the students dramatic instruction, and, rather than putting together an end-of-the-year theatre production, they performed on the most unrelenting stage of all: the real life Scenes that made up each of our Manipulations. I was careful to have each student sign a non-disclosure agreement. I also ensured that they knew next to nothing about each Manipulation.

"Let's set up a party scene," I said. "Get into small groups of two to five, but no talking aloud. I'm going to go from group to group. When I get to your group, you have to start up as if I'm interrupting you in mid-conversation."

The students quickly shuffled around and formed their groups.

"One more thing," I called out. "If I come over to you and say another student's name into your ear, you've go to go over to them, introduce yourself, and try to get their phone number."

"Piece of cake!" the 72 year-old said. *Viejo* is what they all called him—"old man."

"Action!" I said.

I watched the students engage with each other—most were now able to be lively and animated without being overdramatic. One of them would be Diego's new friend. Pancho was just the right age, and he had the confidence and easy demeanor necessary for the job. I walked up to him as he was chatting away.

"I need you for a Manipulation."

He grinned and nodded his head.

"How well can you play soccer?" I asked.

# SEVEN

Elena lived in a brick apartment building in a nice part of town.

A doorman opened the door for me.

"And who might you be calling on?"

"Elena."

"Elena what?"

"I don't know her last name."

The doorman made a face. "Well," he said, "we have two Elenas in this building."

"What are their ages?" I said.

"I would *never* divulge that kind of information."

"Listen," I said, stepping closer to him, "I'm going on a date tonight with an Elena. She lives in this building. She's about my age and has curly, black hair. Give that Elena a call this very moment, or you'll be fired by tomorrow morning at the latest."

The doorman glared at me and went over to the phone. He came back a moment later. "She'll be right down," he said. Then he went over to the elevator and stood beside it. A few minutes later, the doors opened, and the doorman held out his hand to help Elena out.

"And don't you look lovely," he said to her. I shook my head and tried to ignore the way he craned his neck to look at her as she walked toward me.

"For you," I said, handing her the roses. María Paz had insisted.

"Oh, they're beautiful!"

She signaled the doorman over and handed him the flowers. "Put these in water, if you don't mind," she said. "I'll take them up to my apartment when I come home."

I winked at the scowling doorman. Then I opened the door for Elena and followed her out.

I took her to my favorite restaurant, a sparsely decorated place with a wood-fired brick oven and traditional Neapolitan pizzas.

"There's no menu," Elena said.

"They make only the one kind of pizza."

The waitress brought my usual bottle of wine. She knew me by name but had never seen me with company before.

Elena and I chatted about this and that, and, before I knew it, the waitress came by and placed a large pizza between us. It was a thin-crust pie topped with tomato, buffalo mozzarella, basil, and olive oil. I picked up a slice and hoped Elena would not use her fork and knife.

"Do you want to play a game?" Elena said.

"What game?"

"It's called 'There's something you should know about me.'"

Setting my slice down again, I wiped my fingers on my napkin. I could feel the sense of control abandoning me and migrating across the table to this woman who sat there in front of me.

"Let's hear it."

"I have a son," Elena said.

I took care to not slow down my chewing. I had trained myself to never unwillingly show surprise (or any other emotion, really). Every facial expression should be carefully chosen and executed.

"What's the boy's name?"

"Claudio," she said. "He's twelve."

"And his father?"

Elena shrugged and showed me her bare ring finger. I started to ask something, but she interrupted me.

"It's your turn now."

"Something you should know about me," I said.

Elena nodded.

I placed my fingers on the stem of my wineglass and slowly rotated it. "I was married once," I said finally.

"You were married," she said. "And then what?"

Any time I answered that question, I could feel the ground shake and crack, until I was left standing alone on my own little island. I carefully tilted my wineglass until a rivulet of wine ran over the edge and down onto the tablecloth. I looked up. Elena was watching my hands.

"I should get someone to clean this up," I said.

# EIGHT

The evening news and weather report was over. I was standing a block away, waiting for Diego to emerge from the building. He came out and began his usual walk home. I walked a block ahead, and when I got to where Pancho was waiting, I walked by him without a glance. Then I sat on a nearby bench to watch.

Pancho waited until Diego was half a block away and then went over to where a street vendor stood. He bought a bag of peanuts and laughed loudly at something the vendor said. Diego looked over at him. Pancho stepped away from the vendor and fiddled with his change until Diego was a short distance away. He put the wallet in his back pocket, but there was a considerable and deliberate hole in the pocket, and his wallet went straight through, landing right at Diego's feet. Pancho began walking away.

"Hey," Diego said, picking up the wallet. He jogged over to Pancho and tapped him on the shoulder.

"Here," he said. "You dropped this."

Pancho's eyes opened wide, and he made his mouth slightly agape. A little overdone, is what I would say to him at our feedback session later. He thanked

Diego profusely, and then said he'd buy him a beer. He mentioned that he was just on his way to get a drink at the XYZ—where Diego happened to be a regular. Diego agreed, and I sat on the bench until they were out of sight.

Pancho had been instructed to be friendly and outgoing, to pretend he didn't know Diego was on television, and to buy Diego a beer or two. At some point, he was to mention that he was searching for a game of pick-up soccer, in hopes that Diego would invite him to join his Thursday evening game.

The ease with which children and young people make friends makes me envious. On my first day of school, I didn't know a single boy or girl. I went outside during recess, and a boy kicked a soccer ball at me. I kicked it back, and, by the time the bell rang, we were best friends. These days, my friends were all either co-workers or family—neither of which make ideal friends.

# NINE

Waking up in someone else's home is like traveling in a foreign country. I had no idea where anything was or how to behave appropriately. I could hear Elena in the kitchen—opening and closing the refrigerator, humming a little bit to herself. I went to the bathroom to wash up and then walked into the kitchen. Elena was writing something on a piece of paper. She was focused—her eyebrows drawn together in concentration.

"Good morning," I said.

She looked up. "My goodness," she said, coming over to where I was standing. "Your hair is a mess, and you're dressed like a slob." She patted down my hair and tucked my t-shirt into my underwear. Then she stood back to admire her work.

"There's coffee," she said, gesturing towards the table. "Bread, jam, cheese."

She picked up the piece of paper she was writing on when I had walked in. "I was writing you a note. I have to go to work, and I didn't want to wake you up."

"Let's hear it," I said. My voice wasn't fully awake yet.

Elena cleared her throat and held the note out at arm's length. "There's coffee on the table. Help yourself to anything in the fridge. I had fun last night—you were cuddlier than expected."

I frowned. "It was cold."

"I liked it," Elena said.

I was hungry and hadn't slept nearly enough. "Come here," I said, pulling her towards me.

"Absolutely not," she said, kissing me on the cheek and darting away. "I have my makeup on already."

She slipped into her shoes and out the door. I sat down heavily and slathered a slice of bread with jam. I unfolded the newspaper and tried to read, but there was nothing that was capable of holding my attention.

# TEN

Meanwhile, Pancho and Diego played soccer together twice and went to the bar. Upon finding out that Diego was single, Pancho had expressed disbelief and implored him to get a girlfriend so they could spend time as a foursome with Pancho's girlfriend. The stage was set, and I called Laura to tell her the plan.

The XYZ was nothing fancy—just a good place to get a drink. It was fairly well-lit, with a great atmosphere, and they didn't try to drown out your conversations with loud music, either. It was the perfect place to run a Manipulation. I was sitting at a table with one of my students. His name was Marcelo—he was nothing more than a placeholder. Marcelo was sitting with his back to the action so I could look over his shoulder while pretending to converse with him.

Diego and Pancho were sitting at a table not far from mine, working their way through a pitcher of beer. When Pancho got up and walked towards the washroom, I ordered another drink.

"Do you smoke?" I asked Marcelo.

"No."

I went to the vending machine and bought a pack of cigarettes. "You do now," I said, tossing them onto the table.

Marcelo picked up the pack and carefully removed the cellophane wrapper.

Pancho emerged from the washroom and walked back to his table. On the way, he walked by a table of four. I couldn't hear the conversation, but I knew it by heart—I had written it. "So good to see you—it's been too long!" "Hey, why don't you and your friend join us?"

Pancho returned to his table. He yelled something in Diego's ear and pointed at the table of waving strangers.

That evening, on his way to the bar, Diego had walked by a trio of attractive women. They had smiled at him. A man had walked up to him at the bar when he first arrived to compliment him on his extraordinary weather predictions and to thank him for a particular prediction that had—no exaggeration—saved his marriage. All these people were students of mine, helping to prime the conditions for a positive first meeting between Diego and Laura by making sure Diego was in a great mood. We called it "giving someone a good day."

We had given Laura a good day, too. One of my students—*Viejo*—had pretended to be struggling with going up a few steps at the subway. She had offered to help him. He had told her that her generosity was like a sunflower blooming in this barren yard of a city. Outside the bar, she had been stopped by a handsome man who told her he was in a loving relationship and was definitely not trying to make a pass at her but that she was a beautiful and graceful woman, and he just wanted her to know that.

Marcelo was coughing. I handed him my glass of water.

"Okay, okay," I said. "Put it out."

He looked at me through teary eyes.

"Practice at home," I said, "until it looks natural. Then, never smoke one of those things again unless you have to."

"Yes, sir."

One of the strangers at the table of four was Laura. The other three were students of mine—two men and one friendly but deliberately unattractive woman. Laura ignored Diego for the first twenty minutes, as per my instructions. Then she went off to get another beer, and someone who happened to be sitting by Diego took her seat. Everything was going as planned—Laura would return to the table and find her seat taken, and then she would sit by Diego. But, just as she was approaching, Diego peered into his empty glass and got up. He went to the bar and talked to the bartender, who immediately began mixing a drink. Laura went and sat next to Diego's empty seat. She frowned and looked over at me. I avoided eye contact and looked back at Diego. Things had taken a turn for the worse—he was now engaged in a conversation with an attractive woman who had sat down next to him. She kept tossing her hair back and laughing at everything Diego said. I was mentally running through a number of possible approaches to remedy the situation when Diego began walking towards the washroom. I got up and followed him in there.

The washroom was dimly lit and foul-smelling. I slowly washed my hands while Diego peed at the urinal. Our eyes met in the mirror as he pumped soap onto his hand.

"That woman you were talking to," I said.

"Natalia?"

I laughed.

"Sure—if that's what she's calling herself now."

Diego frowned.

"A friend of mine," I said, "actually, the guy I'm having a beer with right now, took her home not too long ago."

"I just met her," Diego said. "Just now."

"I'm not one to talk about these things. I value discretion as much as the next guy."

Diego looked at me curiously.

"But if you're looking for crabs," I said, "I'd suggest you try going to a seafood restaurant instead."

"But she—"

I held up a hand. "Make your own decisions, buddy. I'm just—from one man to another—sharing some information that I'd want to know if I were in your shoes."

He thanked me and left the washroom. I stayed behind for a few seconds. When I returned to my table, I looked over Marcelo's shoulder and saw that Diego had returned to the table. The poor girl was at the bar, pouting, and Laura was happily chatting with Diego.

I closed my notebook and downed my drink. It was time to leave.

# ELEVEN

Elena called me at the office the next day. I was having a rough afternoon.

"You don't sound yourself," she said.

I grunted. "It's nothing."

"Let me cheer you up."

I don't like it when others try to cheer me up, but she persisted.

"I'll come by the office and pick you up in an hour," she said.

I had just stepped out of the building when she drove up. She took one look at my face and started laughing.

"What?" I said, crossly.

She tilted the rearview mirror towards me. I looked into it.

"Sir Frowns-a-lot," she said.

This did not get a smile from me.

"Okay," she said. "This calls for an intervention."

She pulled out into the highway heading out of town.

"Where are we going?" I said.

"We can never know these things," she said.

I wanted to know where we were going and what we were going to do when we got there—but Elena refused to tell me anything. She stopped the car at a truck stop and told me to wait in the car. She came back with a paper bag oily with fried-chicken pieces and another with roasted potatoes. We ate hungrily. I don't think anyone had ever ordered food for me before, and I didn't care for it. But she smiled at me—her wide lips faintly greasy—and I felt something in me give.

"The food does help," I admitted, gnawing on a drumstick.

"The food," she said, "is just the beginning. I took a course in happiness as part of my psychology degree. We took a group of people and measured physiological responses to different situations—we wanted to see what it was that actually made people happy. Eating food was one of the top ones. I'm going to show you another of the ones that had a high response."

"What was number one?" I said.

Elena started the engine. "Music was one of them," she said. "Not number one, but number four or five." She put a cassette into the deck and turned up the volume. I couldn't understand a word they were saying, but the music was cheerful.

"This is in English," I said, accusingly.

Elena shrugged. "You don't have to know what everyone's singing about all the time."

It turned out we were going to the airport. Elena led me to arrivals, where glass doors automatically swept aside and weary travelers were greeted by their loved ones. She left me there without any further explanation. I had resigned myself to giving up control, and did not even ask. I watched couples reuniting, families reconstituting themselves, and friends laughing. Elena returned with a large piece of cardboard. She produced a tube of lipstick from her purse and used it to write her name in block letters on one side of the cardboard. She wrote my name on the other side.

"Here," she said, handing to me. "I'll go first."

And then off she was again. I watched her wind her way through the security line-up, through the metal detector, and then disappear from sight. There was a flight arriving from Buenos Aires, and a trickle of people began emerging from the sliding doors. First the hurried businessmen, not a hair out of place, then the wealthy women, gone to Argentina for a shopping excursion, and then a larger mass of people. I held up my sign expectantly, peering at the doors, and there she was. It was like I was seeing her for the very first time. She swept her gaze from side to side, finally letting her eyes land on me. Her eyes opened wide, and she took in a large breath.

"Elena!" I called out, waving the sign in the air.

"Javier!" she said, stumbling towards me on her high-heeled shoes.

We met in a tremendous embrace, annoyed travelers streaming around us like a river rock—solid and permanent.

"You're here," she said, softly. Here was a woman who had run a Manipulation to cheer me up, and there was not much more I could ask for from someone.

It was my turn next. I was an actor first and foremost, and more at home pretending to meet someone at the airport than actually meeting them there. I went through security and waited for the next flight to arrive. It was the Miami flight, full of bronzed faces and unseasonal clothing. I watched as they did customs and then joined their ranks as they trudged towards arrivals. And there she was again, this time pulling her high-heels off to more easily run towards me, this time letting herself be picked up and swung around. This time I could hardly bring myself to let go—I had released my hold on the side of the swimming pool and grabbed on to her instead.

# TWELVE

The next night, I was taking Elena out to dinner. I drove over to her apartment building and walked into the lobby.

"And who might you be calling on?" said the same doorman as before, with an irritating smile.

"I'm here to see Elena."

"Which of the—"

I interrupted him by holding up a warning finger. "Don't," I said. "Just call her room, and tell her I'm here."

The doorman wheeled around and picked up the phone. He turned his back to me and spoke into it. Then he turned back to face me.

"I'm sorry," said the doorman with a sneer, "but Elena is not able to leave her room right now."

"Let me talk to her."

The doorman picked up the receiver and had a brief conversation with Elena. "If you must," he said, handing me the phone.

"Elena," I said, "I hear you're not well."

"I've received some terrible news." She sounded like she had been crying.

"Let me come up—sometimes it helps to talk about these things."

"I couldn't," she said. "I've been crying, and I'm a mess."

"But Elena . . ."

It continued like this for a few minutes. Eventually, she agreed to let me come up when I offered to get some take-out.

"Tell me about this news," I said, once I had returned with the food.

"I need to eat first," Elena said, her face pale. "I haven't eaten in hours. I feel like I may faint."

I rummaged around her kitchen until I found some plates and cutlery. I filled two glasses with water, arranged the sandwiches on a tray, and brought it out into the small dining area.

Elena ate with a fierce determination, and I chewed slowly, as if hoping to balance things out. We went to the living room and sat down.

"It's about my son," Elena said.

"Claudio," I said.

Elena smiled for the first time since I had arrived.

"Claudio," she repeated. She started to cry.

"I told you Claudio was off at boarding school, right? Well, the program is actually called the 'Intensive Boarding School.' Students are sent off to live in a place called Colonia Alemana. The highest-quality education in the country, it said on the brochure—and it had an endorsement on it from the Minister of Education."

The name sounded familiar. Elena explained that Colonia Alemana was a utopian village in Chile's central valley. It was not far from Santiago—four hours or so by car. It was run by a German, Peter Wenzel.

"A friend of mine whose daughter is part of the program called me this afternoon." Elena said. "Her daughter told her that this Peter takes the boys into his room at night and . . . touches them—does things to them."

She hiccupped and then started crying again. I went to the washroom and brought back some tissue.

"Let's get in my car and drive over to there right now," I said.

Elena shook her head. "They made me sign something when I registered Claudio. Some paper that said that, in order to accelerate his learning, his boarding there would need to be in complete immersion. That is, no visits or contact allowed for the four months of the program. Just letters that they mail us once a week, and that we can reply to. That friend of mine—she drove there a few weeks ago just to visit her daughter, and she was turned down at the gate. She said there were guards with guns."

I tried to remain calm. I thought about Claudio, but only for a second—then I began running through potential Manipulations. There's a hole in every fence, a weak link in every chain. There's always a crack to slip through.

"Can I use your telephone?" I asked.

She showed me to the phone and then left me there. I called Julio and Rodolfo and asked them to come to an emergency meeting tomorrow at noon. I gave Julio the basic facts so that he could do some research.

I went back to the living room, where I found Elena picking at the leftovers.

"Let's play a game," I said.

"I don't—"

"It's called 'There's something you should know about me.'"

Elena looked at me with her eyebrows drawn together. "You start," she said.

"I do have an acting studio," I said. "But I also run an organization called Human Solutions."

Elena raised her eyebrows.

"It's unlisted, unincorporated, and unlicensed. Just a small group of us who work together to make things happen for our clients."

"Things?" Elena said warily.

"Say someone wants a newscaster to fall in love with them," I said, "or their boss to start showing them some respect."

"That doesn't make any sense," she said.

I didn't say anything.

"You didn't tell me this until now?"

"I'll meet with the rest of the team tomorrow first thing and then call you."

Elena shut her eyes tightly.

"Have you called the police?" I asked.

"Not yet," she said.

"Good—just wait till I call you in the morning," I said. Her eyes didn't seem focused properly. "Are you going to be okay?"

Elena looked at me sadly. There was no way she could answer that just yet.

# THIRTEEN

When Julio and Rodolfo arrived at my office the next day, I was already on my third cup of coffee. "Tell us what you found out," I said to Julio. I tried to sit down but found it impossible to be still.

"I spent all morning at the library," Julio said as he flipped through his notes. "Going through microfilm from as far back as the 1960s, and then some recent newspaper and magazine articles. And then the gold mine—a particularly well-researched exposé in *El Mercurio* that got right into the meat of it."

"And?" Rodolfo said.

"Colonia Alemana is a cult," Julio said. I walked over to the window and leaned my head against it.

It was created in 1961 by an ex-Nazi named Peter Wenzel. Uncle Peter, as he asked all the colonists to call him, was an Evangelical preacher who had been kicked out of Germany for founding an orphanage and subsequently molesting the children there. He moved to Chile and bought up an abandoned 4,400-acre property. He brought 10 Germans with him—the original settlers—and, within a couple of years, another 230 Germans, most of Wenzel's original congregation, had flocked to the Colony. These days, there were more than a thousand residents.

The Colony grew exponentially, and it currently housed several apartment complexes, a school, a church, a bakery, and a hydroelectric power station.

"Here's the thing," Julio said, leaning forward. "Has Elena called the police?"

"I told her to wait until she heard from me," I said.

Julio sank back into his chair. "Good," he said. "Because it turns out that our fine dictator, General Pinochet, is pals with Uncle Peter. They've got some sort of cozy relationship—I couldn't find out exactly what's going on, but the exposé suspected something big."

"This one's not for us," Rodolfo said, shaking his head. "This is not some guy who wants his boss to stop harassing him or some woman who wants the weatherman to fall in love with her. This is serious—life or death."

Julio lifted his stack of papers and shook it. "I have to agree with Rodolfo," he said. "I don't care how much this woman is paying us."

"Elena is not just any woman," I said.

They stopped what they were doing and looked at me.

"I like her," I said.

Julio gestured with his hand for me to continue.

"We've been going on dates," I said.

Rodolfo leaned forward. "Have you—"

"Please," I said.

"You're in love with her," Julio said.

I glared at him. "I'll do this one on my own if I have to."

"It's too dangerous," Julio said.

"We won't decide right now," I said. "Why don't we just investigate some more for now?"

Rodolfo shrugged and looked at Julio.

"Call Elena," Julio said finally. "Explain why she shouldn't call the police. I'll see what else I can dig up."

Rodolfo said he would drive out to the village outside the Colony and pose as a reporter. He would ask the villagers about the Colony and explore the surrounding area.

"Do you remember Tibor?" I said.

They nodded.

"I'm going to go have a talk with him."

# FOURTEEN

A few years ago, a man walked into my office. "I want to kill a man," he said.

I held up a hand. "Out."

"Please," he said. "I beg you—let me explain."

I gave him five minutes, and he thanked me profusely. He sat down and crossed his legs at the ankles. Then he began telling me his story.

Tibor was born in 1930 in the Romanian hamlet of Nusfalau. His parents ran the general store. Barrels of beans and flour and potatoes were crammed into every corner. The villagers brought in their empty bottles of vodka, and Tibor's mother refilled them. Tibor's father spent all day in the fields. Evenings, he would pore over the ledger books, calculating profit margins and payments.

"We had goats," Tibor said. "I was nine years old only when I started taking them out to the mountains—first thing in the morning, always with a sandwich in my pocket for lunch. When I was fourteen, I had to start wearing a yellow star on my coat. We all did. It was the most shameful thing that could ever be done to them, my parents said. To me, it was just a star. Then we took a long

47

train ride—my family and all the other people in town who wore stars. We arrived in Mauthausen, and lined up at the gates to a concentration camp in front of a tall man.

"He was like an orchestra conductor, waving his arms this way and that," Tibor said, demonstrating. "When he gestured to his left, the person went to be burned alive. When he gestured to his right, they went to dig holes to bury those people. When it was finally my turn, the tall man hesitated with his hand up. My life was a coda. Then his hand turned to the right. I would be a digger."

Barely surviving on a morsel of bread and a cup of watery soup, Tibor quickly fell ill. One day, while digging, his coughs spattered the white bodies with blood. A guard grabbed him roughly by the collar and took him to see Dr. Koehler.

Tibor was taken into a room that was stark and white. Surgical implements cluttered every surface. The walls were decorated with body parts. A shrunken ear here, a shriveled penis there.

"Dr. Koehler performed operations and amputations without anesthetic on those of us in the concentration camp," Tibor said. "He wanted to see how much pain a person could endure."

I grimaced and shook my head.

"His favorite thing? Injecting victims straight into the heart. With gasoline."

But Tibor knew none of that then. He was fourteen. He was lying on a hard cot. Dr. Koehler put his slight hands on Tibor's head and tied his hands and arms down. Then his feet and legs.

Tibor turned his head. He saw a glass jar full of liquid. The air above the jar was wavy, and he knew what that meant. Dr. Koehler plunged a syringe into the jar and slowly pulled back on the stopper.

Dr. Koehler approached the boy. He raised Tibor's shirt. With his cold fingers, he probed Tibor's chest.

"Did you know that I did this to your father?" he said.

He found the spot he wanted. Between the ribs. Poised the needle above the now-heaving chest.

"And your mother," Dr. Koehler said.

Tibor shut his eyes tight. He tried to think about Nusfalau, before yellow stars and the trains, when it was just soccer and hard candies.

"Then an alarm sounded," Tibor said, "and men rushed into the room."

"The camp was liberated," I said.

"No, no," Tibor said. "It was just an air-raid alarm. But I was untied by a guard, and I ran back to the barracks. The next day, we were liberated."

Tibor was taken to a displaced persons camp. He convinced an official there to issue him a passport and took the next ship out of Europe. The ship steamed across the Atlantic and down the coast of Argentina. It traversed the Strait of Magellan and docked at the Chilean port of Valparaíso.

"I've been living here in Chile for almost forty years," Tibor said. "I own a small corner store a few blocks from here, and I'm a happy man. But, a week ago, I went to the hospital to visit a sick friend of mine, and there was a patient in the bed next to him who looked very familiar. It was him. Dr. Koehler. He didn't even change his name— I had a look at his chart when he was asleep."

He had raged about this to everyone he knew, and someone had told him about Human Solutions. After hearing about his encounter with Dr. Koehler at the concentration camp, I agreed to run a Manipulation for him. It was not an easy decision—but Tibor told me he had changed his mind—he only wanted to *talk* to him. I understood that he was saying this to protect me. The Manipulation was fairly simple. Rodolfo found out who Dr. Koehler's early-morning nurse was, and he mapped out her schedule. Then we got one of my students to spill a vial of blood in the hallway and lie on the ground. When the nurse came by, the student pretended he was a visitor who had slipped on a pool of blood. He held his head and moaned a bit, and the nurse gave him a hasty examination. Then she sent him down to the ER and mopped up the mess.

With those fifteen minutes of added time, Tibor approached Dr. Koehler's bed. He stuffed a sock in the old man's mouth and put tape over it. Dr. Koehler awoke with a start. His eyes opened wide. Tibor tied the man's arms down, and then he sat down on the bed next to Dr. Koehler.

"Remember me?" he said.

Dr. Koehler shook his head.

"How about now?" Tibor said. He opened his bag and pulled out a syringe. He removed it from its plastic casing and then produced a small canister.

"How about now?"

Dr. Koehler shook his head again. Slower this time.

Tibor opened the canister and waved it under the old man's nose. He lowered the tip of the syringe into it and drew back on the plunger. The syringe filled with the liquid. His hands were shaking. Dr. Koehler shut his eyes tightly.

"How about now?"

# FIFTEEN

I went to see Tibor. He still owned and ran the store a few blocks away from my office. The young woman working at the till picked up the phone to tell Tibor I was here to see him. When he came down, he looked worried.

"There's a problem?"

"Let's go for a walk," I said.

We walked out of the store and into a throng of tourists. "There's nothing to worry about," I said. "I just came because I need some help. I'm working on a Manipulation."

"Of course," he said. "For you, I would do anything."

I explained about the Colony. "The way I see it," I said, "this cult is like a concentration camp. You've been there—how am I going to get the boy out?"

Tibor thought about it. "There was a man who was at the camp with me—the only man to get out while I was there. He was on grave-digging duty with me. A group of twenty of us, and two guards. One of the guards took a woman from our group and dragged her into the forest. As soon as they were out of sight, the man who was digging next to me picked up his shovel and threw it at the remaining guard. It knocked the gun out of his hands and hit him in the chest. The man ran over and picked up the shovel. He killed the guard with a blow to the head and put on his uniform. Then he walked out of the camp."

It was afternoon rush hour, and the streets were filling up with bustling pedestrians and gridlocked cars. I looked at my watch.

"You have to walk out of there," Tibor said. "You're not going to get in by force, and you're not going to get out by force. You walk in, you walk out."

# SIXTEEN

I brought a pot of soup and a loaf of bread over to Elena's. She looked like she hadn't eaten or slept.

"I dreamt about Claudio last night," she said.

I didn't want to hear about any dreams.

"Come here," I said. Elena put her head down onto the table. The tablecloth was a mess of soup stains and bread crumbs. I went over to stand behind her, putting my hands on her shoulders.

"Listen," I said. "We're going to get Claudio out of there. We just need to do it right, because there's only one chance. If we drive up there tomorrow and beg and plead and threaten the guards, they'll just turn us away and put Claudio under heavier security. If we call the police, they won't do a thing, because General Pinochet and Uncle Peter have some sort of thing going on. We need to be careful and precise—"

"And quick," Elena interrupted, jerking her head up. She started to cry. I couldn't bear the sight of it.

"To have him taken away from me like this," she said. I handed her a cloth napkin that was resting on the table. She blew her nose noisily.

I thought of the people I had lost—the woman I had married, my father, my mother.

"He would never hurt a fly," Elena said.

That was the problem with letting someone like Elena into my life. They buoy me, and, when they leave, I sink.

"He was such a good boy—slept through the night since the day he was born, ate anything I put in front of him."

She began crying again, this time more uncontrollably. She was in despair. I put my hands on her shoulders and squeezed gently. "Look at me," I said, my voice calm and encouraging. "There, that's it. I want you to let me help you more."

She couldn't seem to catch her breath. "Breathe with me," I said, putting my face close to hers. "Just like that."

I went to get her a glass of water. "Did you eat enough?" She nodded.

"Can I draw you a bath? She nodded again. I was halfway to the washroom when she said something.

"What's that?" I said, coming back into the room.

"Make it hot," she said.

I read the paper while she lay listlessly in the tub. I helped her out, dried her off, and put her in bed.

"Will you stay?" she said.

I took off my pants and shirt and got in. She reached over and turned off the bedside lamp. I turned on my side to face her.

"No, on your back," she said.

I obliged, and she put her head on my shoulder and curled up against me.

"I need you," she said.

I needed her, too.

"You'll bring me my son back?" she whispered.

I felt weightless, like I was floating in the sea.

"I will," I said. But she was already asleep by then.

# SEVENTEEN

"Coffee?" said my secretary, popping her head in. I shook my head without looking at her.

"Please," Julio said.

"As well," Rodolfo said.

We sat there for a moment. "How's she doing?" Julio said.

"About as well as anyone could."

My secretary came back with the coffee. We were silent as she poured and hurried out.

"I came back last night from investigating the Colony," Rodolfo said, stirring sugar into his coffee. "There's no way to break in. They've got a three-meter fence around the perimeter—barbed wire and guards with rifles. Patrolled day and night."

Julio raised his eyebrows. "We can't take this one, Javier," he said firmly.

I shook my head. "I promised her I would get her son back."

"You heard what Rodolfo said—there's no way to break in."

"I'm not breaking in," I said. "I went to speak to Tibor. Here's what he told me: 'You walk in, you walk out.'"

Nobody said anything. My phone rang, but I didn't pick it up.

"I'm walking in," I said. The phone kept ringing. "You can help me if you want—but I'm going in regardless."

Julio drummed his fingers on the table. "You're risking your life for what—some woman you just met?"

I nodded.

"Fine," Rodolfo said, finally, shaking his head.

"We'll have to be very careful," Julio said slowly. "We want you to come out of this alive."

"You walk in there," Rodolfo said, "and then what?"

"Is there anything in here . . . ?" I patted Julio's notes.

Julio took off his glasses and began cleaning them. "You might be tempted to avoid Uncle Peter," he said, in his professorial tone. "He's a cruel and abusive man— but you've got to get as close to him as possible. Give him admiration and flattery, but not too much. That's the way these leaders are—the Hitlers, the Stalins, the Maos, the Pinochets. They attract gushing admirers, and you've got to be something other than that. Give him some admiration, sure, but also some honesty, and, whatever you do, don't act afraid. Find Claudio, find someone you can trust, and cozy up to Uncle Peter."

Julio stopped in mid-gesture. He dropped his hand and shook his head. "But it's the stupidest thing you've ever done."

"How much do you know about Claudio?" Rodolfo said.

I called Elena and put her on speakerphone.

"We need your help," I said. "I'm going in there, and I need to know everything about Claudio. What he looks like, what he likes to do, how he should be approached."

"He's a happy boy—he's confident and has a big smile. He plays the clarinet," Elena said. "In one of his earlier letters, he said that he plays in the orchestra there."

I wrote this down.

"He likes playing almost any sport, but especially soccer."

Julio cleared his throat. "Elena, this is Julio—Javier is going to need to convince Claudio that you sent him. Is there something he can say—something only *you* would know?"

Elena thought about this for a minute. "You just tell him that Papo needs someone to cover his ears."

"Pardon?"

"His Papo—that's what he calls his teddy bear that he's had since he was born. When he was little, he used to cover Papo's ears whenever there was a scary bit in his bedtime story."

Elena sounded like she was very close to crying. I had more questions for her, but now was not the right time. There was much to prepare

"The day after tomorrow," I said, after hanging up the phone, "I need someone to drop me off at the Colony."

"I can do it," Rodolfo said.

"So help me God, if anything happens to you," Julio said.

# EIGHTEEN

Rodolfo picked me up at noon on Saturday. I had been up all night.

We went by Julio's house and honked the horn. He hurried out—his wife poked her head out the window and waved at us. It took forever to get out of Santiago. There was not much traffic, but we sat for long seconds at stoplights. Soldiers stood attentively at street corners, clinging to their guns. This was General Pinochet's own Manipulation—keep us all afraid, remind us constantly that we are being watched and monitored.

"It's not too late to turn back," Julio said.

I opened the window and let the wind pull noisily into the car.

Julio stretched his hand across to the seat and rested it on my shoulder. I didn't move out from under it.

As we moved further from the city centre, high-rises became suburban houses and then battered apartment buildings, subsidized housing, and, finally, cardboard slums. Soon the clutter of five million people vanished and was replaced by long expanses of fields and mountains. Trellised grapevines butted up against the highway, and I leaned back and tried to relax.

"How are you feeling?" Julio asked. None of us had spoken in a while, and his voice scraped.

"I'm not," I said.

"Once you get in there," Rodolfo said, "you need to become a detective. Stay sharp and alert. Eyes open, ears open—be gathering information every minute of every hour. Follow your instincts, and stay calm."

Rodolfo steered his station wagon off the highway. He turned onto a dirt road. *Colonia Alemana*, a brightly coloured sign read. There were freshly plowed fields left and right. Rodolfo pulled the vehicle over to the side of the road.

"It's just up there," he said. "Better if they don't see the car."

I nodded, and we all climbed out of the car. I picked up my small suitcase and looked at Julio and Rodolfo.

"If this doesn't work . . . ," I said.

I couldn't continue. Julio stepped over to where I was standing and gave me a hug. I had not been hugged by another man since my dad had passed away. "I'll see you soon, okay?" he said.

Rodolfo pulled me into his arms. His beard sifted through my shirt and scratched my shoulder. "I swear to God" he said, "if you don't make it back, I'm going to sleep with your sister."

We agreed that they would drive to this very location every Sunday at noon and stay there until two. I thumped the hood of the car and started walking down the road.

"Javier," Julio called out.

I turned around.

"Don't forget," he said. "You walk in, you walk out."

The Colony was not very far—ten minutes at the most. I came to a tall cement wall that was heavily crowned with barbed wire. I heard someone yell, and a guard appeared from a small booth and slowly walked over to me.

"What are you doing here?" he demanded.

"At long last," I said, looking up at the sky. "I have come home."

I was taken to a small room and told to sit and wait. The walls were crowded with bucolic scenes from the Colony—children splashing in a lake, a group of men erecting a barn, three flour-dusted women kneading dough—and many of a man who was presumably Uncle Peter. He wore sunglasses in all but one of the pictures. In that one picture, he was giving the camera his profile, staring off into the distance.

My stomach sat as heavily as a cannonball—the last time I had been this nervous was in elementary school. I was in third grade and a finalist in the annual speech contest. I ate nothing for breakfast that morning and sat on the stage in my school uniform (grey pants, light-blue shirt, navy vest, loosened tie) while the first- and second-grade contestants went up to the podium. When it was my turn, I climbed down from the chair and made my way over to the microphone. I squinted into the bright lights until I found my father. He was smiling and pointing at his cheeks, urging me to smile. "If you *act* like you're relaxed," he had said that morning, "then you'll *be* relaxed." I slumped my shoulders and forced a grin. I evacuated any trace of anxiety from my body language, just like my father had shown me. Then I began speaking.

There was a flurry of conversation from outside, and I returned to my chair. A group of people entered the room. Two guards led the way, taking positions on either side of the door. They were followed by three men, who all stood before me. One of them, the oldest, leaned on a thick cane.

"Tell us your name, boy," he said. I had not been called "boy" in two decades.

"My name is Javier," I said. I stood up to shake their hands and introduce myself—immediately, one of the guards took a step forward and readjusted the grip on his rifle.

"Relax," the old man said to me. "What brings you here, Javier?"

"I've been unhappy with life for as long as I can remember," I said. "I live in the capital, where you can't throw a stone without hitting a sinner. When I heard about Colonia Alemana, I knew that I had finally found my way home."

One of the men blew his nose loudly into a handkerchief. I looked at him.

"Hay fever," he said.

"Everyone here has to work," said the old man. "Some of us are carpenters, some of us are cooks, some of us are teachers. What do you bring to the Colony?"

"Ah," I said, pretending to have to think about it. "Well, I did run an acting school for many years—I could teach people how to act. Children, perhaps? We could put on plays every now and then."

The old man creased his brow. He cleared his throat. "I think a theatrical performance would not be a terrible idea," he said. "We will have to ask Uncle Peter, of course."

They stepped back and conferred with each other in whispers.

"You will join us for supper," said the old man. "And then you will meet Uncle Peter. He will decide whether you will be accepted into the Colony"

"Thank you, gentlemen," I said, bowing my head. "You are saving my life."

"I hope you are well and certain of your decision to join the Colony," Hay Fever said. "Because once you've walked in these gates, there's no walking out. The guards are only to let people out in extreme circumstances—a fire, etc."

"There's no need to go anywhere," the old man said. He gestured all around us. "Everything you could ever need is right here."

The men walked out, and I was left alone with the two guards.

"Supper is in fifteen minutes," said one of them. "In the dining hall. Don't be late."

They hoisted their rifles and walked out of the room.

"Wait," I called after them. "Where's the dining hall?"

One of them turned and spat on the ground. "You can't miss it—just follow anyone."

I was left alone in the room again. First place—I had beaten the fifth-grader, the fourth-grader, and the first- and second- and third-graders.

# NINETEEN

I walked down the wide, unpaved road that cut through the center of the Colony. Men and women emerged from brick apartment buildings that appeared to be segregated by gender. They were dressed the way I imagined German peasants might traditionally dress: the men in thick pants and suspenders over white shirts, the women in modest dresses and headscarves.

The colonists wore docile expressions for the most part, and they did not speak to each other much. The men and women were of varying ages, but there was not a child in sight.

The dining hall was a large wooden building, church-like in appearance. I followed the colonists into the room and into a lineup that ended at a long table where food was doled out. It was not so different from what I had experienced as a schoolboy.

There was a large blackboard at the front of the room, and, as the colonists streamed in, some of them went up to the blackboard and wrote down a name. After a few minutes of waiting in line, I looked up to see a commotion at the door. All of the children had arrived. They marched in, hushed and admonished by their supervising adults, and hurried over to the food line.

I got to the front of the line and craned my neck to see what I would be eating. "What is this?" I asked the man who was standing in front of me. He pretended not to hear me. I turned to speak to whoever was behind me but was interrupted by the sound of microphone feedback.

A man stood at the blackboard. He was tall and wiry, with thinning gray hair. He wore oversized aviator sunglasses and an impeccable white suit—which made him stand out in contrast to the uniformly old-fashioned clothes worn by the Colonists. It was unmistakably Uncle Peter.

"We have many names today," he said calmly into the microphone.

The colonists nodded obediently. They looked at him with what I took to be a combination of fear and worship.

"Starting at the top," Uncle Peter said. "We have Alejandra Goethe."

A woman stood up, blushing fiercely, and bowed her head.

"Yes, Uncle Peter," she said.

"Your name is on the sinner's list," Uncle Peter said. "Why don't you tell us why it's there?"

Alejandra looked around at the women sitting near her. They averted their eyes and concentrated on eating. "I don't know, Uncle Peter."

"NONSENSE!" Uncle Peter yelled. There was feedback again, and I winced. "Someone put your name on the list, and I demand to know why!"

Alejandra's hands shook as she pulled at the sleeves of her dress. "I tempted a man," she whispered.

The clatter of cutlery abruptly died down, and the colonists leaned forward.

"That's better," Uncle Peter said, calm again. "How did you tempt him?"

"I untied my hair just as he was walking by," Alejandra said, so quietly that everyone in the room seemed to hold their breath. "And pushed my breasts up against my shirt."

Uncle Peter commanded her to sit down. He railed against temptation for a few minutes. Then he ran out of steam and proceeded to the next name on the list. He worked his way through the long list of names, urging men and women of all ages to confess to lying, tempting, misbehaving, and many other variations of sinning, some of which I had never heard of but seemed to be accepted by everyone. I was less shocked by Uncle Peter's denouncements than by the betrayal and suspicion that he had produced in the colonists. I found myself becoming anxious and uneasy, and was reminded of General Pinochet's similar strategy—asking Chileans to turn in their friends and neighbors, even their family members, if they exhibited what he called unpatriotic tendencies.

I listened to Uncle Peter's voice rising and falling, his shifting cadence, and the varying speed at which he spoke. This was a man who had been a preacher for most of his adult life and a man who loved to hear the sound of his own voice.

When he was done, the colonists began taking their plates to the kitchen, and a team of men and women began cleaning tables and washing dishes. Everyone began filing out of the hall, and I was approached by a guard.

"Follow me," he said.

I followed him out of the hall. We marched down the road and back to the small room where I had been interviewed by the three men. The guard waved his gun at the chair and told me to sit. I thought of what Julio had told me—to get as close to Uncle Peter as possible with admiration but also with honesty and a lack of fear.

I heard voices outside the room, and I stood up and walked over to the photographs. It was where I wanted to be when Uncle Peter walked in. I chose a picture of him and pretended to study it. The door creaked open. I turned around slowly.

"Oil this door," Uncle Peter said to the guard.

The guard hurried off.

"Please," Uncle Peter said, gesturing towards the chair, "have a seat."

I didn't want to have him standing over me while I sat—it would create the type of power dynamic that Uncle Peter seemed to thrive on.

"I was admiring these photographs," I said, ignoring his request. "Magnificent."

I walked over to Uncle Peter and stuck my hand out.

"I'm Javier. It's a pleasure and an honour."

He shook my hand and gave a pleasant, forced smile.

"Please," he said again, gesturing towards the chair.

"Thank you," I said, "but my knees. They are stiff from all the sitting at supper. And I must say, what a delightful meal. The sauerkraut alone had enough goodness to feed a man for a lifetime."

"I do like the sauerkraut myself," he admitted grudgingly.

"You are a much talked about man in my community," I said.

"What community is that?" he demanded.

I named one of the more prominent Evangelical churches in Santiago.

"Is Pastor Sotomayor still working there?"

"I'm not sure who was there before," I said, "But now it's Pastor Morales." Julio had done his research.

Uncle Peter leaned back, satisfied.

"He mentions you frequently in his sermons," I said. "And I have spoken to others at the church. Everyone agrees that what you have built here is nothing short of a Utopia."

"I will not ask why you want to live here," Uncle Peter said. "Everyone wants to—especially those who are unfortunate enough to live in a sinful city like Santiago."

Uncle Peter faced me and made a show of slowly removing his sunglasses. He had one regular eye and one glass eye. The glass eye looked not unlike a cloudy marble. I didn't flinch—in fact, I forced out a yawn.

"How can you contribute to the Colony?"

I told him about my idea of putting together an acting group. He frowned at me for a moment. "The children here *do* need to learn more about the history of the Colony," Uncle Peter said slowly.

"Of course—and of its founder," I said gesturing at him.

Uncle Peter mentioned that artistic endeavors should happen outside of working hours only and that I would need to work during the day to help the Colony run smoothly.

"We have a library," he said. "Our librarian is at the end of his tenure. He is 84 years old and needs to pass on his knowledge. You have come along at just the right time."

I agreed to work at the library and said that I would need to meet with him somewhat regularly to conduct a series of interviews in order to write up the play about his life.

Uncle Peter nodded. "Mornings, you will work in the kitchen, making breakfast," he said. "After breakfast, you will report to the library."

I nodded.

"Oh, and one more thing," he said. "Don't talk to anyone here about what's going on out there in the rest of the world. Not a word."

"Very well, sir."

"Don't call me that," he snapped. "Call me Uncle Peter."

# TWENTY

I was taken by a guard to my sleeping quarters. We went into one of several nondescript apartment buildings and walked up the stairs to the third floor. The guard rifled through a round of keys on his belt and found the right one. He unlocked the door, pushed it open, and turned sharply to leave.

"You almost forgot," I said, sticking out my hand. "The keys."

The guard looked at me incredulously. Then he barked out a laugh and put his face up close to mine. "These doors don't lock for people like you," he said. His breath stank of sauerkraut, but I stood my ground. "They lock when I decide or when Uncle Peter decides. That's it. Understand?"

I shrugged. "Oh sure," I said breezily—I wasn't going to give him any satisfaction. "I should turn in now," I said. "Big day tomorrow. First day of school."

The guard shook his head and left without another word.

I pushed the door open. The room was clean and sparsely furnished. There was a single bed, neatly made, and a nightstand with a lamp and a Bible on it. In the corner, there was a straight-backed wooden chair. The only piece of decoration was a small framed portrait of Uncle Peter that hung above the bed. I closed the door and placed my suitcase on the floor. The bed was lumpy and firm. I crawled in and turned this way and that, trying to get comfortable. When I was finally still, a series of sounds began leaking into the room. A man sped through a Hail Mary—his voice a loud monotone—then another, and another, and several more. When he had finished and I was thanking the same Mary for that small miracle, I discovered that his droning had drowned out a far more distressing sound—that of a man crying. He was subdued at first, but, before long, his heaves reached a sobbing crescendo, and I pressed a pillow down onto my head to block it out.

At some point, I must have fallen asleep, because, the next thing I knew, I was awoken by a stern shouting. I hauled myself up on the creaky bed and squinted at the doorway. It was still dark out.

"Your pants," the man said. It was the guard from last night.

I nodded, waiting for him to continue.

"And your shirts," he said. He dropped a stack of folded black pants and white shirts onto the floor. Then he dangled down a pair of suspenders and let those fall, too.

"Be at the dining hall in five minutes," he said.

"Five minutes?" I said, rubbing my face.

"That's not much time to get ready—is it?"

I didn't respond.

"I thought of waking you up ten minutes ago," he said, "but you looked so peaceful there, sleeping."

The thought that this man had watched me sleep for the last ten minutes was both disturbing and terrifying.

"You must be a special kind of man," I said, "if watching other men sleep is your idea of fun."

He kicked furiously at the pile of pants and shirts, scattering them all over the room.

"Your room is a mess," he said evenly. "You've got clothes everywhere. If it's a mess again, I'll report you to Uncle Peter."

He turned abruptly and left. I put on the clothes—they were all on the large side—and made my way over to the washroom. I shaved in front of a warped mirror and washed my face with cold water. I tried to repress the anxiety I was feeling and replace it with a sense of purpose. I needed to find Claudio and get us both out of the Colony—but there were a series of smaller goals that would lead to that, and I needed to focus on these.

The kitchen behind the dining hall was buzzing with activity when I walked in. A dozen or so men and women were washing and dicing and frying. I stood in the doorway, alone, feeling just like I had when I first arrived at that party my sister had taken me to. Stay calm, stay positive. I took a deep breath and smiled. I stopped a woman who was walking by and asked her who was in charge. She pointed at a large woman—old enough to be my mother—who was peering into a walk-in cooler.

"Good morning," I said, as I approached her.

"It would be a better morning if you could butcher a pig and take care of our bacon shortage."

I smiled and stuck out my hand. "My name is Javier. I'm here to help with breakfast."

"Anita," she said. "First thing that needs to be done is cleaning the tables. Fill a bucket with bleach and warm water and find a rag. Every table needs to be wiped down. There's mouse droppings and spider webs and all those things that happen overnight."

The kitchen was warm from all the moving bodies and stovetops and ovens. The dining hall, on the other hand, was cold and empty. I took my bucket of warm, bleachy water and set it down on a table. I dipped the rag into it and then swished it across the table—first in straight lines but then in a more easy, circular motion. I had not done very much physical work in recent years.

My first taste of it was when I was twelve, and my father thought it would be good for me to spend the summer away from the city. It was right after my mother had died, and my father was hardly getting out of bed most days. He sent me off to my aunt's house; she lived alone on a farm in the southern part of the country. The bus ride was long and uneventful—my first time traveling alone—but the change in geography as we rolled down narrow roads was magnificent. The vineyards of the central region became lakes and waterfalls, and my nose was glued to the window for hours. My aunt needed help on the farm, and I was more than happy to pitch in. It felt good to be needed and to work on concrete tasks that were quantifiable. For one glorious summer, there was no more pretending to be happy around my father, no more putting on short one-man skits just to try to get him to smile, but rather picking bushels of green beans and pints of strawberries for hours on end. I worked until my back was sore and my fingers cramped.

I alternated rags, leaving one to soak while I used the other, and made my way down the rows of long tables. The light in the room began to change, and I went to look out one of the windows. The sun was slowly working its way over the Andes. Elena would just be getting up now. She would be drinking two cups of coffee and reading the newspaper. I wanted her to look at the clock and hurry out the door. To drive out past the city limits. And I—I wanted to arrive, to see my name written in large block letters, to push through a crowd of suitcase-draggers and fall into her arms.

I found Anita scrambling eggs. "I'm done with the tables," I said. She looked at the clock on the wall.

"Great," she said. "Go help that man slicing tomatoes."

I walked over to the man and told him I was sent over to help. The man wordlessly handed me a knife and pushed a cutting board towards me. There was a series of wooden tomato crates stacked several feet high. I reached for a large one and began slicing. The serrated knife was as sharp as any knife I had ever used—after a while, the weight of the blade alone seemed to be doing the work for me.

"You've been doing the breakfasts long?" I said.

The man looked up quickly from his slicing and then back down. It was not going to be very easy to gather information from these colonists.

I tried a different tack. "The way you're slicing those— you're very good at it."

The man did not look up—he frowned and then nodded curtly.

We sliced tomatoes in utter silence for the next half an hour, until we were interrupted by the clanging of a bell.

Over the next ten minutes, there was a furious rush in the kitchen. People darted about, helping others finish up their tasks. Trays and bowls and hot plates were hurriedly shuttled out to the dining hall and over to the serving table. I wandered over to an enormous pot and went to peek inside it.

"I need someone to serve that," Anita said.

I looked up. "What is it?"

It was oatmeal.

"Just stand here," Anita said, "and use this ladle to serve anyone who holds a bowl out to you."

She left, and a river of colonists began to flow into the room. They armed themselves with trays and silverware and formed a line at the serving table. The first one in line—an unusually tall, bearded man—picked up a bowl.

"Good morning," I said cheerfully.

He ducked his head and held his bowl out. I ladled a generous amount of oatmeal into it. He peered down into his bowl, then held it out for me again. I heaped more into his bowl, and, from then on, I did not stop doling out oatmeal until the line of colonists had trickled down to nothing. Anita came out and told me to hurry up and grab some food. I went back into the kitchen and found the staff circled around a table full of food. I grabbed a plate and discovered that I was famished. Soon, my plate was full of fruit, scrambled eggs, sausages, toast, and sliced tomatoes. No oatmeal.

I peeked out into the dining hall. The majority of the colonists were chatting comfortably in hushed tones while they ate their breakfasts. There's an easy way of relating to others that I had never quite picked up. For me, each social interaction is fraught with subtext and body language— everyone was always after something; that much I was sure of. Maybe there was something about removing all external circumstances that simplified the way colonists were able to interact with each other. By having their daily lives pared down to the most basic level, these colonists were able to form relationships that were not weighted by discrepancies in social status, the intricacies of office politics, or the uncertainties of sexual tension. Perhaps it was my line of work—acting, in one form or another— that placed layer upon layer of complexity upon each and every interpersonal relationship, making it impossible for me to converse plainly with another human. Plainly, without an agenda, intention, or motive.

I ate a forkful of eggs. Someone brought in a rack of dirty dishes from the dining hall, and a group of people hurried over to their dish-washing positions. I put my plate down and went over to Anita.

"What am I supposed to be doing?" I said.

"Sit down," she said. "Eat. Then you're off duty."

I nodded gratefully and found a corner in which to sit and eat my breakfast. Then I brushed the crumbs off my freshly starched white shirt and pants. I walked out into the bright sunshine and was nearly run over by a stampeding herd of young girls.

# TWENTY-ONE

"Field mice!" called the adult who was hurrying after them. "Behave yourselves!"

I stood still, letting the children pass. I scanned their faces, but they looked to be younger than Claudio. I found a guard marching down the road and asked him for directions to the library. He pointed at a wood-shingled house in the near distance. I slowly made my way over to it. The exterior of the house was a faded yellow with white trim. There was a front porch with a pair of rocking chairs on it. I was startled to find a man sitting quietly in one of the chairs.

"I didn't see you there," I said.

"I don't have my hearing aid in, so, if you're talking—I can't hear you."

I walked up the steps and over to the chair. I mimed a wave and mouthed the word *hello*.

"Sit down," said the old man. "I'm just joking—I can hear fine. I'm Ernesto, the librarian. You must be my new chicken-walker."

"Chicken-walker?"

"I keep some chickens out back," Ernesto said. "They need exercise, so every morning I take them for a walk."

I wasn't sure if he was joking again or not.

"I'm not joking," he said.

"I'm not your new chicken-walker," I said firmly. "Uncle Peter sent me to help you with the library."

Ernesto shrugged. "I'll show you around the library, and then we'll go for a walk," he declared. He put his hands on his knees and hoisted himself up onto his feet. He was a wiry old man—the kind who performs creaky calisthenics every morning before eating a large bowl of oatmeal and prunes.

I followed him into the library. There were large, sturdy bookshelves lining the walls and some additional shelves clustered around one side of the room. We went out through a back door and into the backyard. There was a chicken coop on one end—a small, red house with a tin roof. Ernesto walked out to the coop, and the chickens clambered over to him. He retrieved a pair of sticks that had been secured to the wall of the coop and held one out to me. The stick was a few feet long and had a small rubber worm tied firmly to one end. Ernesto demonstrated how the chickens would follow the dangling worm. This carrot-and-stick technique seemed to work well, and we went off on our walk, the chickens clucking busily as they chased after the unattainable worms.

We had not traveled far when the same group of young girls hurried by. Their supervising adult was still scolding them, "Field mice! Stay together!"

One of the chickens next to me began clucking anxiously.

"Pick her up!" Ernesto said, pointing. "She's going to make a run for it."

I had no idea how to pick up a chicken. I handed Ernesto my worm stick and squatted down. I grabbed the chicken the same way I would grab a soccer ball—one hand on each side—and she flapped her wings mightily in my face.

I let go—by this point the girls had passed, and the chicken looked more anxious about my clumsiness than anything else.

"You have to pin the wings down with your hands when you pick one up," Ernesto said. "Or they flap them."

"What was that woman saying 'field mice' for?" I asked.

"Those are the Field Mice. The way Uncle Peter's got things set up here is that people are divided up by gender and by age."

"Oh?" I said, hoping to elicit more information.

"At first, everyone is part of 'The Babies,' up until they're six years old. They're taken away from their parents as soon as they're born and raised by nurses in the hospital. At six, the boys join 'The Wedges,' and the girls join 'The Field Mice.' At fifteen, the boys join 'The Army of Salvation,' and the girls join 'The Dragons,' and so on."

"How does Uncle Peter convince parents to give up their children at birth?" I said.

"You some sort of reporter or something?"

"It's just a curious thing—to take away someone's child," I said, thinking instantly of Elena and Claudio.

"You're not the usual type of person who shows up at the Colony."

I shrugged.

"But the chickens like you, and they're not often wrong about this sort of thing."

"So how does he do it—get the parents to give up their babies?"

"Oh," he said, "you'll see. It's all just one big . . . trick, I guess."

"A manipulation."

"Sure, a manipulation. He generates fear, builds distrust among the colonists, that sort of thing."

I looked over at Ernesto.

"Keep your eyes on the chickens," he cautioned. I turned my head back and jerked the stick away just before a chicken was able to clamp its beak down onto the rubber worm.

"Once they find out the worm is made of rubber, the whole thing is over," Ernesto said.

We walked for a little while longer and then made our way back to the library. When we returned, there was a guard waiting outside for us. "Uncle Peter needs to see you," he said to me.

I followed the guard at a fast clip down the road.

"What does he want to see me about?" I asked. The guard ignored me. Before long, we arrived at a large and ornate house. I was shown to a waiting room. A young boy—one of The Army of Salvation?—was sitting at a desk. He looked to be working on a school worksheet. I thought of my secretary. When the boy saw me, he jumped up and went over to one of the closed doors. He knocked on it and peeked his head in. After he came back to his desk, he told me that Uncle Peter would be ready in just a minute.

There was something about waiting for a person in a waiting room that made one feel utterly powerless. I wondered if Uncle Peter was indeed busy, and I felt a pang of guilt for having made Laura and all the others wait while I pretended to be busy. I was also reminded of having had to wait outside the principal's office when I was young—I could hear the faint rumbling of my father's voice and the short but declarative utterances of the much-feared principal, Ms. Cortés. I scooted my chair closer to the door—when the secretary looked up from her typewriter, I stopped moving and looked around innocently. Still, I couldn't make out what they were saying. Then the phone rang, and the secretary listened briefly before hurrying out of the room, and I boldly got up and pressed my ear against the door.

". . . learned it from you?" Ms. Cortes said.

"Florencia—may I call you that?"

She must have nodded, because my father repeated her name once more.

"Florencia," he said, "Javier is at the age where his brain is starting to work in novel ways—neurons and synapses are making new connections, and it would be unrealistic to expect the boy to ignore the brilliant ideas that pop into his head."

"That is no excuse for tricking the other boys out of their lunch money, Mr. Gonzalez, and you—"

"With all due respect, Florencia, Javier did not trick anybody out of anything—he merely devised an ingenious game that the boys could play. Surely you'd rather have a group of boys doing that rather than smoking cigarettes in the washroom?"

The game my father was referring to was one that I had invented that week. It was a competition among my group of friends, to see who could be the first to get a teacher to dispose of our lunch tray for us. We had all put our lunch money on the table, and, one by one, we found a teacher roaming around the cafeteria and tried. One boy tried feigning a leg injury (the gym teacher, who he had stupidly approached, sent him to the nurse), and another boy went up to our history teacher and asked her to hold his tray while he tied his shoe. She nodded at an empty table nearby, and the boy reluctantly put the tray down there. When it was my turn, I waited until it was almost time for the bell to ring, and I made my way over to the science teacher. I told him we had a bet going at our table, trying to figure out what weighed more: a soccer ball or my lunch tray. I handed him the tray, and, as the bell rang, I ran off, leaving him holding the tray. I told him I was off to find a soccer ball, but I went back to the table, scooped up the money, and went off to class— only to get called into the principal's office the very next period. Someone must have told.

There was much rustling of chairs, and my father was asking Florencia if she would join him for dinner sometime. Mortified, I hurried back to my chair and put on a remorseful face.

"Uncle Peter is ready to see you."

I looked up—the boy was standing there. I thanked him and went into Uncle Peter's office. It was a spectacular affair, filled with heavy, turn-of-the-century furniture and thick rugs. An elegant glass chandelier dangled from the ceiling. The usual photographs of the Colony and its founder cluttered the walls. Uncle Peter was sitting at his desk, fingering an unlit cigar.

"Tell me how your first day has been," he demanded.

I nodded vigorously. "This place—everyone has been kind and welcoming."

He leaned forward and lit the cigar, puffing on it. "I didn't ask you to tell me something I already know," puff, puff, "I asked how your day was."

"It was excellent," I said, forcing a smile. "Everything I hoped for, and more."

Uncle Peter stared out the window. The man was an expert at making anyone feel as insignificant as a flea.

"I wanted to ask," I continued, "about one of the guards—"

He snapped back to attention. "You're an actor."

I agreed with him.

"I need an actor for a special project."

"Of course," I said. "And what is it that I will be acting in?"

Uncle Peter waved my question away. "There is a guard waiting outside—do exactly as he says."

# TWENTY-TWO

I was sitting in a tethered rowboat with a guard, the smallest of them all. His ears had been taped into points, and he wore green from head to toe.

"This is too tight," the guard complained, pulling at the small hat that was tied under his chin. He glared at me, as if this whole thing was my idea.

I had been given an itchy white beard and a floppy, red sleeping cap. There was a pillow stuffed under my shirt. The guard looked at his watch.

"In three minutes," he said.

I put my hand in the water. It was cold—glacier run-off—but not turbulent. The riverbank was heavily vegetated, but, up ahead, I could see a clearing. That's where Uncle Peter would be waiting with all the children.

"You see," Uncle Peter had said to me in his office, "Christmas is still a month away, and all the children want to talk about is Santa Claus this and presents that."

"Christmas," I said, shaking my head.

"And I am nauseated from hearing about this. They have forgotten about Jesus and the real meaning of Christmas."

I asked him how this had happened.

"This year, we brought in some new children through a boarding-school program. They brought with them disgusting tales of gifts and a fat man in red and white. So we're going to give them what they want. We're going to give them Mr. Santa Claus himself. And who better to play the role than a real actor!"

It was a very "Human Solutions" way of dealing with the problem—I had to give him that. Uncle Peter was going to gather the children together after lunch and lead them on a walk through the forest and over to the river.

The rowboat was moving now, and I held on to the sides. We gathered speed, and, before long, I could see Uncle Peter over by the clearing. The children were gathered around him—there seemed to be more than a hundred of them. I squinted to see if I could pick out Claudio. I knew that, with such a large population, it would be some time before I would be able to find Claudio—but every passing moment filled me with a growing sense of urgency.

Uncle Peter pointed at me, and the children began jumping up and down and waving their arms.

"Santa! Santa!" they yelled. "Bring us our presents!"

I stood up shakily.

"Ho Ho Ho!"

"Louder," demanded the elf.

"HO HO HO!"

Then I saw Uncle Peter pull a small handgun out from under his belt. He showed it to the children and leveled it at me. The ensuing gunshot was louder than

I expected—echoing off the water. Uncle Peter had promised that he would fire far above my head, but it was, nonetheless, terrifying. I finally remembered to clutch at my belly and double over.

"Fall off," whispered the elf.

"I know," I said. "But the cold."

The elf grabbed both sides of the rowboat and leaned hard to one side. I stumbled overboard, hitting the water with an icy thud that pulled the air out of my lungs. I floated downstream on my back with my eyes closed. I could hear the cries of children moving farther and farther away.

"Okay, okay," said the elf. He had been rowing his boat alongside me. "We're far enough now."

I sputtered into an upright position and went to pull myself up the side of the vessel.

"No, no," he said, poking me away with an oar. "Just swim to the riverbank there."

I was sick of this elf telling me what to do, but I dutifully swam to the riverbank and pulled myself out of the water. I struggled out of my wet costume and left it on the ground for him to pick up.

# TWENTY-THREE

By the time I was showered and dressed, it was almost time for dinner. I made my way over to the library. Ernesto was sitting at his desk.

I straightened a book that was sticking out on one of the shelves. "I'm putting on a play," I said. "Uncle Peter asked me to—a play about his life."

Ernesto chuckled and shook his head.

"You know what he had me do this afternoon?" I said.

I told him about my performance as Santa Claus.

"That man," Ernesto said, frowning.

"It's true," I said, "but the cleverness of it—that counts for something in my book. If nothing else, he deserves a small amount of grudging admiration."

"Admiration?" Ernesto said, curiously. "He emotionally scars a group of children by feigning murder, and you want me to *admire* him?"

Any man who was this strongly opposed to Uncle Peter was at least somewhat trustworthy. If nothing else, he would provide information to help me plan the escape.

"Anyway, it's going to be a children's performance. I need to find some boys and girls who are interested."

"There are sometimes announcements at dinnertime. After the blackboard."

The dinner bell rang. Ernesto and I walked over to the dining hall and got in line. There was whitefish and scalloped potatoes and coleslaw. I loaded up my tray and followed Ernesto to one of the benches.

"Attention!" The microphone crackled to life. Uncle Peter stared at us sternly. "There are many names on the list today. Let's get started."

The first name on the list was Eugenia Castro's. She had large hands and a farmer's build.

"Why is your name on the list, dear?" Uncle Peter asked sweetly.

Eugenia started to cry. She was wringing her hands, and they were starting to turn red.

"I don't have all day," Uncle Peter said.

"If you just—"

"I DON'T HAVE ALL DAY!"

I tried to eat without making a sound. Ernesto was looking down at his food and mechanically bringing up each forkful. He seemed to be completely removed from the present situation.

Eugenia cleared her throat and wiped her eyes. "I revealed to my boy that I'm his mother," she said.

Uncle Peter put down the microphone and wiped his brow with a handkerchief. He shook his head in disbelief. He lifted his hands in resignation and looked around at the other colonists.

"I must be mistaken," he said, picking up the microphone. "It sounded like you said that you told your son that you are his mother."

Eugenia nodded and stared straight ahead, pulling her thick shoulders back defiantly. I was sitting close enough to see that her legs were shaking and her breaths were quick and shallow. Uncle Peter signaled a pair of guards, and they slowly advanced upon Eugenia. The colonists yelled and screamed for her to be punished. Someone threw a bread roll at her, but she batted it out of the air and did not break her posture.

"Her son was born five years ago," whispered Ernesto. "He has Down Syndrome."

"So she can't talk to him?" I asked.

"She can talk to him—she just can't tell him she's his mother. As you know, babies are taken away from their parents and raised separately. A child is meant to be raised by the community as a whole, without ever knowing the identity of their mother or father. They have only one relative here—an uncle."

I looked over at Eugenia. She was crying. One of the guards held up a potato sack and cut a hole for Eugenia's head. He pushed the sack down over her head, then cut holes for both her arms to go through.

I leaned towards Ernesto. He explained that all traitors and rebels were forced to wear clothing that would set them apart from the other colonists. The men wore red shirts and white trousers, and the women wore potato sacks. They were mistreated and abused by the other colonists. It sounded like a great strategy for making sure everyone stayed in line—a constant reminder of what could happen to you at any moment.

"It sounds to me," Uncle Peter said, "like you're a person who talks too much—would you say that's true?"

Eugenia kept her head down. She looked terrified.

"Let me tell you what we do to people who can't keep their mouth shut. Sometimes we do nothing."

Eugenia's shoulders sagged gratefully. There were murmurs amongst the colonists.

"BUT OTHER TIMES," Uncle Peter continued and then dropped his voice down to a whisper. "We sew their mouth shut!"

There was a collective gasp. Eugenia squeezed her eyes shut. Uncle Peter took a leisurely sip of water. His capacity for cruelty was astounding.

"Tell you what," he said. "Why don't we head over to the clinic after dinner?" He said this as casually as if he were suggesting they go for coffee sometime.

Uncle Peter went through the rest of the names on the sinner's blackboard—at one point, a young boy confessed to praying that Santa Claus would be resurrected like Jesus. Ernesto shot me a pointed look, and it occurred to me that I had seldom witnessed the collateral damage of my own Manipulations.

When Uncle Peter was done, I hurried over and asked if I might make an announcement.

"It's about the play," I said.

"Then do it already," he said impatiently.

"Hello," I said into the microphone. "My name is Javier. I'm new here. I'll be putting on a children's play a month from now, so, if you want to participate, you can write your name on this piece of paper."

There seemed to be no interest whatsoever. Uncle Peter took the microphone back. "It will be a play about my life," he said. Still nothing. "Rehearsals will take place during evening prayer."

This did the trick. A boy stood up and came over, and then another boy, and then a girl, and, before long, there were enough children on the list to put on a production.

"Our first rehearsal will be very soon!" I called out.

I looked at the sign-up sheet. Claudio's name was not on it. I remembered what Elena had told me about her son playing clarinet in the orchestra.

"Who runs the orchestra here?" I asked Ernesto.

"The orchestra," he repeated, looking around the room. "That woman over there."

I walked over to the woman and waited a few feet away until she finished a conversation she was having. Then I tapped her on the shoulder and introduced myself. Her name was Greta. She was a stern-looking woman with a heavy German accent.

"You make the play?" Greta asked.

"Yes, yes," I said enthusiastically. "You're right."

"Good," she said, turning away.

"Wait," I said. "The play needs music. Music." I mimed someone playing a violin.

"Music, yah," she said impatiently.

"Can your orchestra do music for play?"

She made a face as if she had eaten a rancid walnut.

"It is for Uncle Peter, this play," I said. "It is about his life in Germany. I need German music."

She looked at me.

"Uncle Peter wants," I said.

Greta exhaled sharply through her nose. "I can do music."

I thanked her profusely and left before she could change her mind. I returned to the table and began to tell Ernesto about my conversation with Greta. We were interrupted by a young boy who ran up and tapped me on the shoulder.

"Did you want to be in the play, too?" I said.

"Uncle Peter says you should come to his office tomorrow after lunch to interview him for the play."

"Very well."

The boy ran off. I turned to Ernesto. "Uncle Peter has messenger boys?"

Ernesto motioned for me to follow him. "I need to close up the chicken coop for the night," Ernesto said. "Or else the fox will get them." We took our trays to the front of the room and left the dining hall.

"You sure you want to hear about the messenger boys?" Ernesto said. "It's the kind of thing you might wish you didn't know—unless you were an undercover reporter or something along those lines." He winked at me.

I grinned. It seemed like a good idea to let him continue to believe that.

"That's all right with me," he said. "I want the world to know what goes on in here."

The messenger boys were called Sprinters. Being made a Sprinter was the highest honour for boys at the colony. Uncle Peter would use them to communicate with colonists who were on opposite ends of the colony, hence the name. He also had them carefully trained to help him with many menial personal tasks.

"What kind of tasks?" I said.

"Holding the phone to his ear," Ernesto said. "Helping him put his clothes on."

I frowned, and Ernesto looked away. We closed up the chicken coop in silence.

# TWENTY-FOUR

I rolled out of bed before sunrise and pulled on my regulation pants and shirt. I hooked my suspenders over my shoulders and went to wash up. Not having to choose what clothes to wear every day was an unexpected pleasure. Maybe there was something to be said for occasionally giving up control. Maybe there was a freedom in that—a freedom that came from a lack of freedom.

I peered into the mirror and ran a comb through my hair. I patted some water onto it and carefully parted it on the opposite side than usual. It was a trick I had been using for years to help me get into character. It was, in fact, a relic from the time when Human Solutions was created.

There was a flurry of activity when I arrived at the kitchen. Anita saw me and waved me over. "Eggs," she said. "They're in the walk-in cooler. Get a box and separate them into yolks and whites."

"I'll do the tables first," I said.

Anita shook her head. "We need to get going on these pancakes. Then you can do the tables."

"Yolks and whites," I confirmed, nodding.

I repeated that phrase over and over in my head, yolks and whites, yolks and whites. It became my mantra for the next few minutes—while I found the eggs (there were 252 in a box) and cleared some counter space for the project.

I found two oversized bowls and put a compost pail down by my feet. Then I stood there for a moment and thought about how to go about doing the separating. Anita came over.

"I've got a trick for doing this," she said. She picked up an egg and cracked it on the edge of the stainless steel counter. She pulled the shell apart into two halves and held these upright over one of the bowls. Then she shuttled the yolk from one eggshell fragment to the other, back and forth, letting the whites slip down into the bowl. When all that was left was yolk, she moved over to the other bowl and dropped the yolk into it.

The task grew easier as I worked my way through the layers of eggs in the box. After a while, I was able to pull my mind away from the egg task and towards the more complicated task of figuring out how to escape from the Colony. There were enough sharp knives in the kitchen to fight an army—but I knew nothing of knife fighting. The guards were younger, stronger, and more armed than I was. I would need to outsmart them.

Someone hurried over and traded my half-filled bowls for empty ones. I could hear the griddle spitting on the other side of the kitchen and Anita calling out instructions. Then I discovered that there were no more eggs in the box. I cleaned up my work station and went out into the dining hall, but someone had already done the tables. They were shiny and slowly drying.

The breakfast bell rang. I found a ladle and set myself up at the oatmeal-serving station. People began flooding into the dining hall, and I began dishing out oatmeal to everyone who wanted it and to those who were waffling, too. "It's good for you," I assured them.

Then Eugenia came up the front of the line. She looked miserable. A thick, black thread had been stitched across her lips. There was just enough space for her to put a straw in there. Her face was blotchy, and droplets of blood still clung to the thread. She looked at me helplessly and gestured at her sewn lips.

"Just one second," I said. I roped a fellow kitchen worker into filling in for me at the oatmeal station, and I went to find Anita. She was already working on lunch. I explained that we needed to make some sort of blended drink for Eugenia.

"That poor girl," Anita said. "I'll take care of it."

After the rest of the colonists had sat down to eat, I went back into the kitchen and ate my breakfast. There were still more pancakes being made at the grill—for those who would be coming back for seconds and thirds—and I helped myself to a couple of them. I put a large pat of butter on top and some homemade cherry syrup.

"What do you think?" Anita said, appearing beside me.

My mouth was full, but I closed my eyes and nodded. Anita patted my shoulder affectionately. "Good job today."

I swallowed. "Did Eugenia get something to eat?"

Anita nodded.

"That man," she said, frowning.

When I made my way over to the library, Ernesto was nowhere to be found. I stood at his desk and called his name out. He came out from a room marked "Library Staff Only" and greeted me.

"What did you think of the pancakes?" I said.

"Heavenly."

"I'm going to tell you the secret to making a good pancake."

"I can't be trusted with secrets."

"You have to separate the eggs into yolks and whites."

Ernesto sat down at his desk. "Thank you for that," he said.

"What were you doing in that room?" I asked. "Library Staff Only."

"Library things."

"What kind of library things?"

Ernesto looked at me. "Can you be trusted?"

"Probably not."

"Good," he said, motioning for me to follow him. "You'll want to include this in your article."

He pushed the door open and flicked a light switch. I stepped into the room. There were shelves from floor to ceiling. Every square inch was covered in video tapes and audio cassettes.

"Pornography," I said.

Ernesto gave me a look. "It's news reports," he said. "All of them. Every once in a while, Uncle Peter decides to play the colonists a news report, just so they can see how bad things are out in the world."

"Things are not so bad out there."

"They are once these tapes have been edited."

Ernesto explained that, every few weeks, one of Uncle Peter's confidants would come into the room to splice together a television newscast. The newscasts would invariably paint a picture of an outside world that was devastated by disease, plague, and starvation.

"Why all the audio cassettes?" I asked.

"Before we had a television."

I pulled a video off the shelf and looked at the label. "September 16, 1970—Starvation in Africa / Increased Rates of Suicide." I picked out another. "March 12, 1981—Earthquake / Hanta Virus in Southern Chile."

I couldn't help but admire the brilliance of the Manipulation: take an outside voice (the most trusted voice of all, that of a newscaster), and gently coerce it into transmitting the message that you want sent out. Simple, yet effective.

There was a television set in the far corner of the room with two VCRs attached to it and a radio with two tape decks. I started to get a kernel of an idea.

# TWENTY-FIVE

We went out to the coop and rounded up the chickens. It was a cold, clear morning, and we walked briskly. The chickens ducked and bobbed their heads in time to the rubber worms' movements.

"How did you end up at the Colony?" I asked.

"Hold this," Ernesto said, handing me his worm stick. He tucked his shirt into his pants and rolled up a drooping cuff. One of his suspenders straps had twisted, and he flattened it out. I handed him back the stick.

"My wife died three years ago," he said. "Her name was Angela. She was born in the same German town as Uncle Peter—in Troisdorf. He was an odd child, but they were good friends. They would race each other after school every day and wander around in the woods. When they finished school, she moved to Berlin and got a job at a bakery. She met a young man one night at an art show, and, within three months, they were married."

"You," I said.

"Not me," Ernesto said. "An artist. He was from France. He read poetry to her in a language that she could not understand and smoked cigarettes with his paint-stained fingers. They weren't married for more than a year before he started sleeping with other women. One night when he didn't come home, she piled all his belongings into their bathtub and turned on the tap. By the time it had filled up with water, she had packed up her bag. She turned the tap off and left their apartment. There was a train leaving for Troisdorf in the morning, so she slept on the hard wooden benches at the train station. She was in Troisdorf for a week before she ran into Uncle Peter. He told Angela he was going on an adventure. He had bought land in Chile and was going to start a community there. Angela wanted to be as far away from anywhere as she could, and so she asked if she could go. He told her they would be leaving in a week's time. And, so, a week later, they took a train down to Frankfurt, picking up Uncle Peter's followers on the way down."

"What followers?"

"While my Angela was flitting around the Berlin art scene, Uncle Peter was roving across the countryside with a guitar and a heart full of sermons. He started a small congregation and soon had accumulated a few hundred followers. He even built an orphanage for children who had lost their parents in the war. Everything was going quite well, until someone discovered that he was molesting the children."

A group of guards was approaching us, marching in synchrony down the road.

"Then you want to make sure that, within each genre, you place the books in alphabetical order," Ernesto said.

"And that's *within* each genre?" I asked. "Well, that does make some—Good morning!"

The guards ignored us and walked past. When they were sufficiently far, Ernesto spat on the ground.

I nodded.

"Angela had not been in Troisdorf long enough to find out about these accusations, so there she was, sitting next to Uncle Peter on a train that was rapidly filling up with followers. They steamed across France and down to Spain, until they reached their final destination—the port of Seville."

"Seville . . .," I repeated. Something important had happened there, I remembered vaguely from my high school history class.

"Seville," Ernesto said. "Where Ferdinand Magellan left from. But more importantly, the birthplace of one Ernesto Villegas."

I remembered—Magellan was the first person to sail around the world.

We had circled around the Colony and returned to the library. The chickens were returned to their coop, and Ernesto and I went into the library.

"The Field Mice are coming by for a storytime," Ernesto said. "You can sit with them and watch, and, when I'm done, I'll ask you to read them a story."

We went over to where the children's books lived. Ernesto picked out a few and told me to pick one. I had never read to a child before and was not sure how it was done. I told him so, but he dismissed my concerns with a wave of his hand. Then there was a stampede of footsteps at the door, and Ernesto lay down on the pillowed ground of the "Children's Corner" and pretended to sleep.

"Let them in, will you?" he said, opening one eye.

I went to the door and opened it. A group of twenty or so young girls shrieked and skittered by me.

"You're not the librarian!" one of the girls said accusingly.

"I found him," a girl behind me called out. "But he's sleeping again!"

The girls threw themselves onto Ernesto and tried to wake him up. Their teacher gave me a weary look and told me she would be back to pick them up. I turned around in time to see Ernesto open one eye and then another, and give an exaggerated yawn.

"You will not *believe* what I was just dreaming about," he said to the girls. This seemed to be some sort of routine, because they immediately climbed off him and went to sit quietly over on the pillows. Ernesto pushed himself up, and his voice dropped to a whisper.

# TWENTY-SIX

"Once upon a time," Ernesto said, "there was a young boy named Enrique. He lived on a small island that was part of a group of islands called the Philippines. Enrique was fourteen years old, and he had four little brothers and three little sisters."

"I want a little sister," said one of the girls, waving her hand in the air. Ernesto smiled and motioned for her to put her hand down.

"One day," he continued, "there was a storm, and a big wave came from the ocean and destroyed all of his family's land. They had very little to begin with, and, now, they had nothing at all. Enrique's father—who was not a very nice man—announced one night, as they all had bowls of rice for dinner, that he would be going to town the next day and selling one of them as a slave."

"What's a slave?" said one of the girls.

Ernesto paused for a moment. "A slave is somebody who has to do everything someone else tells them to do."

Some of the girls looked confused.

"When you're someone's slave," Ernesto said, "you have to clean between their toes when they're in the bathtub, and you have to wear whatever they tell you to wear, and, if they want you to jump up and down for them, you have to do that, too.

"The next day, Enrique's father woke him up early in the morning. Enrique hugged each of his brothers and sisters, and the last person he said goodbye to was his mother. They both cried, and Enrique promised that he would be back someday. Then his father pulled him by the arm and they left, in the early morning dark, to walk to town. It was a long ways to town, and Enrique was very tired by the time they arrived. His father fed him a banana and told him to look alive and strong. Then he gave him to a woman who looked Enrique over and nodded. The woman told Enrique to stand in a lineup with a group of other boys—most of them older. Soon a man appeared and walked down the line. Sometimes he would ask a boy to show him their teeth or to make a muscle with their arm. The man chose a boy from the lineup and gave some coins to the woman. Another man appeared and did the same, and then another. Nobody looked twice at Enrique, and, before long, almost all of the boys were gone. Then a small man appeared.

"'Who can understand what I'm saying?' said the man in Spanish. Enrique looked around at the boys who stood next to him. None of them seemed to understand, but Enrique did. 'I can,' he said timidly. The man walked over to Enrique. He asked him if he had ever been on a boat, and Enrique said that he had, many times. This was not true.

"That afternoon, the man took Enrique to his ship and left him there with the other sailors. Enrique learned about sailing from the other men. They were impressed at how easily he could climb the long wooden beams that held up the sails. They sailed for a long time—across the Indian Ocean, down under Africa, and up the Atlantic Ocean—until they got to a country called Spain. They day after they arrived, a man came on board the ship. He was tall and had a large sea captain's hat on his head. All of the crew members were called up to the deck to meet the man. His name was Ferdinand Magellan. He had been asked by the King and Queen of Spain to see if he could find a way to sail a ship around the world. He needed many people from different countries to come with him on this trip, so that they could help him communicate in other languages.

"Enrique said that he would go, and he and some of the other crew members followed Ferdinand Magellan back to his own ship. They lived on his ship for the next week—it had been anchored right near land. One evening, Enrique was mopping the deck when Ferdinand Magellan called him over. 'We're leaving on our big trip tomorrow,' he said to him. 'Yes, captain,' said Enrique. 'We will be sailing for many days,' said Ferdinand, 'but if everything goes as planned, then, someday, we will return to your home.' 'Can I ask a question?' said Enrique. Ferdinand Magellan nodded. 'Somebody told me we are sailing that way,' he said, pointing towards the west. 'That's right,' said Ferdinand Magellan. 'But my home is that way,' he said, pointing east. Ferdinand Magellan put his hand on the boy's shoulder and walked with him over to a barrel of apples. He picked one up and showed it to the boy.

"'The world is round,' Ferdinand Magellan said, 'like this apple.' Enrique looked at it but did not say a word. 'It doesn't matter if you go west or east—soon enough, you will arrive at the same place.' Enrique knew that the world could not be round. If it were round, like Ferdinand Magellan said it was, then everyone would be falling off of it all the time. 'I'm afraid,' he said, 'about what's going to happen if we go to the edge of the world.' Ferdinand Magellan looked at him—he realized then that Enrique was just a boy. Like many grown men, Ferdinand Magellan was not quite sure how to speak to boys. He thought for a moment and then said, 'Tell me, boy, what does fear feel like?' Enrique looked down. 'I couldn't say, captain.' 'Does it make your heart go faster?' 'It does.' 'Does it make you breathe harder?' 'It does, captain.' A man came by asking to speak to Ferdinand Magellan—Ferdinand Magellan said he'd be ready in just a minute. 'Now, let me ask you another question. What does excitement feel like?' 'I couldn't say, captain.' 'Would you say it makes you breathe harder?' 'Yes, captain.' 'And what else does it do?' 'It makes my heart go faster.' Ferdinand Magellan took his large sea captain's hat off his head and placed it on Enrique's. It hung down and covered his eyes. 'You're the captain,' he said. 'You get to decide if what you're feeling is fear or excitement. To your body, they're the same thing, anyhow.' Enrique nodded, and, when Ferdinand Magellan put the hat back on his own head, the boy was smiling. 'Get some rest, sailor—' Ferdinand Magellan said, 'tomorrow is a big day.'

"The ship left port early the next morning, and they were on the open ocean for many weeks without seeing any land. One day, Enrique was sitting at the very top of the very tallest sail—he was the lookout. He saw a seagull fly by, and then another, and then he saw something in the far distance. 'Land!' he shouted. Finally, the ship had reached the shores of South America and the country of Argentina."

All of the girls turned to look at a small girl with bright-red hair. "Pepa!" they cried out.

"I'm from Argentina," Pepa whispered to Ernesto, apologetically.

"It was a big and beautiful country, full of beaches and mountains and lakes and Pepas," Ernesto said. The girls giggled, and Pepa hid her face in a pillow.

"They sailed down the coast of Argentina, hoping to find a way to the other side of the continent. When they were at the very bottom of South America, they found a narrow pass where they could cross. It is a place that is now called the Strait of Magellan. As they slowly tried to squeeze their ship through the passage, a storm came out of nowhere, and large waves began pushing and pulling at the ship. One minute, Enrique was standing on the ship, his eyes wide and afraid, and, the next, he found himself flying through the air and landing in the freezing cold water. He swallowed a mouthful of water and coughed, and then he saw that he was not far from land. He took a deep breath and swam as hard as he could.

"When he pulled himself up onto the rocks, he turned around and saw that some of the other men were in the water, and they were swimming over to him. It was a cold night, and those who had survived built a fire. It was December, and it was almost 500 years ago, and they were in Chile. The next morning, they woke up to a bright sun and found the ship floating happily in the water. It had been only slightly damaged—some men had even managed to stay on board. The explorers then continued, sailing up the coast of Chile, and then across the biggest ocean of all, the Pacific Ocean. The temperature grew warmer, and the smell of the air reminded Enrique of home. Soon, they began sailing by tiny islands, and Ferdinand Magellan called Enrique to his cabin.

"'According to your papers, you are from the biggest island in the Philippines,' Ferdinand Magellan said. 'Is that right?' Enrique nodded. 'Tomorrow we will be arriving at that very place. You will be the first person to ever have sailed around the world. And, tomorrow, you will be a free man again—free to go home to your family.' Enrique could not think of a single thing to say. 'Thank you, sir,' he said, finally.

"Sure enough, the next day, the ship put its anchor down, and a crew of men went over on a rowboat to buy some food and trade some goods. Enrique said goodbye to Ferdinand Magellan and the other sailors, and he got into the rowboat. As soon as they reached land, Enrique began walking home. It was a shorter walk than he remembered, and soon he could see his house in the distance. 'Mama,' he yelled, and he began to run. His mother was in the kitchen. She was preparing lunch—everyone else was outside, working in the fields. She hurried outside, and there he was, running, running, running, and then finally collapsing into her waiting arms. 'I sailed around the world,' said Enrique. 'Come inside—' said his mother, 'you must be hungry.'"

# TWENTY-SEVEN

The girls clapped at the happy ending, and Ernesto took a comical bow.

"And now," he said, "I'd like to introduce you to our new friend, Javier. He's going to read you a story."

It was an impossible act to follow, but I bravely got up in front of the girls and read them a book about a little duck that gets lost in the city.

"You're going too fast," said one of the girls. She had long, tight braids on either side of her head. I slowed down.

"Those who are on that side can't see any of the pictures," she said, moments later.

I finished the story, and Ernesto told the girls they could pick out some books to borrow or just read on the pillows. I went over to the pigtailed girl and asked her name.

"Maca," she said.

"Maca," I said, "how would you like to be in my play?"

She was sitting cross-legged on the floor, flipping through a book.

"That's fine," she said, "but I'm pretty busy right now reading this book."

The lunch bell rang, and the Field Mice's teacher appeared to take her charges to the dining hall.

"Field Mice," she called out. "Don't forget to clean up!"

The girls ran around in a frenzy, tidying things up. They hurried out the door, and Ernesto fell into his chair. He pulled out a handkerchief from his pocket and wiped his forehead. Then he found a glass of water on his desk and took a long drink.

We went to the dining hall. The lineup had dwindled down to a few latecomers, and, before long, we had trays full of pasta primavera and three-bean salad. I ate with my head down, like Ernesto. I took my tray to the wash station and walked with Ernesto back to the library to pick up some materials. This was to be my first interview with Uncle Peter, and I didn't want to be late.

I didn't have to wait long outside the office before the boy sitting at the desk told me that Uncle Peter was ready for me. There was sunlight streaming in through the oversized window, and Uncle Peter was rifling through a stack of papers.

"I don't have much time for this," he said briskly, "so we'll be doing a short session—just something for you to get started on the script."

I produced a slim tape recorder that I had found in the Library Staff Only room and a small notebook.

"I hope you don't mind," I said. "I don't write fast enough."

Uncle Peter looked at the tape recorder warily.

"What if I give you the tapes as soon as I am done writing up the play?" I said.

Uncle Peter thought for a moment and then waved his hand impatiently. "That's fine," he said. I loaded a tape into the deck and turned it on.

"Let's start at the beginning," I said. "You were born in Germany?"

Uncle Peter went on a rambling narrative about growing up in the quaint town of Troisdorf, including a lengthy description of his mother and their close relationship. I asked easy questions and listened attentively—Julio had insisted that I needed to get Uncle Peter to like me, and I've found that people tend to like those who will listen to them talk about themselves. Uncle Peter had joined the army at a young age, where he sustained an injury that gave him a glass eye and an honorable discharge. He later began working as a youth leader at the Evangelical Church. "It was at the Church that I first discovered my ability to touch people," he said.

I frowned.

"I traveled around—oh, that beautiful German countryside!—playing my guitar and spreading the Lord's word. Every time I stopped somewhere, I would pick up a handful of followers. I was like a magnet, and these people were iron filings. They could not stay away—I was a father to them all."

"And your own father?" I said. "I don't think you've mentioned him yet."

Uncle Peter looked at the clock. "Ach," he said, "you've taken enough of my time."

I thanked him and went out into the bright afternoon. A group of young boys appeared from around the corner, kicking a soccer ball and yelling about what the teams would be. They seemed to be Claudio's age, but they ran past me before I had time to try to identify him.

This near-encounter generated some anxiety—I needed to find Claudio and let him know I was here to help. I walked down the road until I encountered a passing guard, and I told him I needed to find Greta, the orchestra director. He looked at me blankly.

"Uncle Peter has asked me to speak to her," I said importantly. The guard took a step back and had a brief conversation into his walkie-talkie.

"She's out in the field," said the guard. "Picking green beans."

He gave me directions on how to get to there and then continued on his way. The fields were not far from the main road—I soon found myself lost in long rows of carefully weeded crops and apple trees heavy with immature fruit. I shielded my eyes from the sun and watched a large group of colonists harvest tomatoes. I looked around and tried to pick out where the green beans might be. A passing colonist pointed me in the right direction, and I finally found Greta hiding beneath an oversized floppy hat and a long-sleeved dress. I reached into her basket and pulled out a handful of green beans.

"These look delicious," I said.

"Put it back," Greta said sternly. "We are having our baskets to weigh. If I don't do enough, there is more picking."

I apologized and dropped the beans back into their basket. "When is your next rehearsal?"

"Today, in the night."

"I would like to come by to tell the children about the play."

"We have to practice."

"Uncle Peter asked me," I said. I was quickly finding that invoking Uncle Peter's name any time I was met with resistance worked wonders.

"You can come in the first part." She gave me directions on how to get to the rehearsal room and told me to be there at seven o'clock sharp. Then she turned her back to me and continued picking beans.

I returned to the library and went into the Library Staff Only room to work on converting the tape into the beginning of a play. Ernesto occasionally came by to listen, and he would invariably chuckle and point out discrepancies between what his wife had told him and what Uncle Peter had told me. When I got to the part about how Uncle Peter had injured his eye at war—hence the glass eye—Ernesto threw his hands up in the air and turned to leave the room. I paused the tape player.

"All right," I said. "Let's hear it."

"Hear what?"

"The real story of how Uncle Peter got his glass eye."

He shook his head. "I'm not sure you're ready."

# TWENTY-EIGHT

It took me several tries to find the building. By the time I walked into the rehearsal room, it was well past seven o'clock. I paused outside the door, listening to the strains of a familiar but hard-to-place melody. The band came to a sudden halt.

"Trumpets," Greta said firmly, "is not good. This is too loud, and not together." She loudly hummed the melody they were supposed to be playing. I nudged the door open and peeked my head through. Greta turned to look at me. All the musicians followed her gaze.

"I'm sorry I'm late," I said. "I got lost. Please, continue with your rehearsal. I'll sit here quietly and watch."

"Quietly," Greta said, frowning.

I lifted a chair from a tall stack and unfolded it. Greta had the band take it from the very beginning—after only a couple of measures, she rapped her baton against the music stand and began pleading with the flutes to stick to the tempo of the piece.

I looked over at the clarinets and immediately spotted Claudio. He was small for his age and wore glasses. He looked like his mother. He was focused intently on Greta and on the sheet music that crowded the stand he was

127

sharing with a fellow clarinetist. Greta gave the band a few minutes to drain their spit valves and rest their mouths. I got up and walked over to her.

"They sound wonderful," I said.

"This band is very terrible."

"I can see them improving even in the little time I have sat here."

Greta looked at me suspiciously.

"I need three of your boys to play a very small part in my play. They will be on stage for just a few minutes, and then they will return to the band."

"You can take all of my three trumpets," she said. "They are hurting my ears."

I looked over to see if the trumpeters had heard Greta. They were not paying any attention to us.

"I need smaller boys," I said. "For the costumes that I have. How about that one, that one, and that one."

"That one is the good clarinet."

"You have taught him well. That is exactly why we need him on stage. It will make Uncle Peter so very happy. He likes him a lot." I looked at Greta meaningfully.

She looked away. "Go talk with them now," she said. "Then leave. We need to make rehearsal."

I went to sit down. Greta got the band's attention and told the three boys to come over and talk to me. They came over, and I briefly explained that I would need them for the play. I did not offer much detail as to the roles they would be playing, and they seemed moderately interested.

"You can go now," I said.

Greta was focused on the band—I grabbed Claudio's arm and motioned for him to hold on a second. The two other boys left. I turned him by his arm so that his back was facing the band and they would not be able to look at his face.

"What?" Claudio said, looking scared. He was nothing like the happy, confident boy that his mother had described.

"Claudio, my name is Javier," I said. I tried to look as trustworthy and inoffensive as possible.

"I'm a friend of your mother's. She sent me to get you out of here."

I stopped for a moment to let this sink in. Claudio did not say a word.

"I asked your mother what I could say to make you believe that she had sent me. She said I should mention that your Papo needs someone to cover his ears."

"Papo," the boy whispered. He looked like he might start to cry.

"Now, listen," I said. "You can't tell anyone about this. Not a single person. If people find out I'm here to help you get out, they will do very bad things to me—and to you. I'm going to try to get us out of here soon, but it'll take me some time. I need you to be patient and to do exactly what I tell you to do. We're going to get out—I promise."

Claudio looked wary. This was a lot of information to process. I told him to get back to the band and to try to act normal. He nodded and began to turn around.

"One more thing," I said. "Are you a Sprinter?"

Claudio shook his head. "I don't want to be a Sprinter," he said. "One of the boys said that Uncle Peter does things to the Sprinters in his room at night."

I looked at him seriously. "I'm not going to let anyone do anything to you."

Claudio looked down. He had a look on his face like he wished he could believe me. He returned to his seat and picked up his clarinet. He flexed his fingers and joined the rest of the band in mid-song.

# TWENTY-NINE

I woke up early the next morning. After a shower, I went for a walk. I left the main core of the Colony and took a narrow path which cut across empty fields. I walked the perimeter for a while, examining the unscalable fence and looking for gaps. There were none. I went a little further and came across a large, white clapboard church. It sagged in places, but the stained glass windows were all intact. There were three steps leading up to the door. I tried it—but it was locked.

I walked back, taking the long way past Uncle Peter's office. I went around the back of the building and found what I was looking for—a window into his office, just out of reach.

The kitchen was in full swing when I arrived. Anita grabbed my arm and pulled me out of the kitchen and into an underground root cellar. It was cool and dimly lit, and I followed Anita closely. She pointed at a barrel of potatoes and handed me a wooden crate.

"Fill the crate with potatoes," she said, "Then scrub them, and slice them thin as you can."

It took some time to get the hard-caked dirt off the potatoes. Then I got to work slicing them.

When the breakfast bell rang, I went out to the oatmeal station. Greta was the first in line. She came by and held out her bowl.

"We made omelettes today," I said.

She did not say a word.

"With potatoes and peppers and basil. Just down that way on the end of that table."

"Oatmeal," she said, "is for good strong bowel."

Ernesto was in line behind her. He winked at me over her head. I gave her a large serving and urged her one more time to try the omelette.

"And for you, sir?"

"Don't *you* look like a man who's been up for hours," Ernesto said, holding his bowl out.

I looked around—all the older colonists were in my oatmeal line, and the younger ones were clamoring for omelets. Beside the oatmeal, we kept large bowls of dried fruit and nuts. I watched Ernesto spoon some chopped hazelnuts and dried apricots into his bowl.

When everyone had their breakfast, I went back into the kitchen and served myself a portion of omelet and a small bowl of oatmeal. I was middle-aged.

Ernesto was cleaning out the chicken coop when I arrived.

"They look like they're ready for their walk," I said.

Ernesto agreed and handed me my worm stick. We set out again, this time on a longer walk down to the river. The chickens clambered after us, clucking quietly to themselves and occasionally in conversation.

"Where was I?" Ernesto said.

"Your wife Angela was on a train with Uncle Peter and his followers. They had just reached the port of Seville."

"I was born in Seville at the turn of the century, in a very small house. My mother gave birth to seven girls, and then to me. I left home as soon as I could—I was sixteen—and began working as a longshoreman. It was easy enough, and I enjoyed the uncomplicated way that a group of men relate to each other. I married a woman who worked at a factory by the docks, but she died giving birth to our only child. The child died a few months later, and I more or less shut down for a decade.

"One day, long after I had given up on ever loving or being loved again, a group of Germans arrived on a train. They were to board a vessel bound for South America. We were still working on some repairs to the ship, and the group stayed in a small inn near the docks. One of the women came by every day to watch us work—that was Angela. The other longshoremen yelled things out, catcalls and vulgar propositions, and I told them to leave her be, and couldn't they see how sad she looked? I had picked up bits and pieces of several languages while at the docks, and, one day, I approached Angela and asked in broken German if she would join me for a drink. She agreed, and, by the time the sun came up the next morning, we were in love.

"Two weeks later the ship was ready to sail, and Angela insisted that I come with her. I would have gone anywhere for her. It wasn't until we were on the open seas that I began speaking to her fellow travelers. Everyone seemed to be crazy in one way or another but none more so than the leader."

# THIRTY

By this time, we had returned from our walk and put the chickens back in their coop. Ernesto settled down to some librarian duties, and I volunteered to sweep. As I carefully built up piles of dust, I thought about the brief moments Elena and I had spent together—they were not many, and I was not sure we loved each other, but it seemed possible that we might someday, and that was enough for me. Ernesto and Angela had loved each other quickly, and perhaps we could, too.

Ernesto and I worked in silence for the better part of an hour, until the lunch bell rang. The dining hall was louder than I had ever seen it—the colonists seemed energized and in unusually high spirits. I asked Ernesto what was going on. He shrugged. "Nine times out of ten, this means Uncle Peter is away."

Sure enough, there was no sign of Uncle Peter, and no blackboard. Lunch was potato salad with a hearty bean and vegetable stew. I ate hungrily and went back for seconds. When I returned, Ernesto got up and picked up his tray. "Take the afternoon off," he said. "There's not much that needs to be done at the library. Go read a book, or do some work in the fields."

It was a warm and clear afternoon. I made my way over to the long, orderly rows of crops and approached the first colonist I saw. He was a man of about my age and was intently weeding something. He was using mostly his hands, but, occasionally, he would scrape at the soil with a small trowel.

"What's that you're weeding?" I asked.

"Carrots."

"Wouldn't you like a hand with that?"

The man shook his head tightly.

"What if I start all the way at the other end of the bed?"

"I guess," he said.

"Great. And what should I be doing, exactly?"

"Pull out everything but these," he said, gesturing at the small, feathery carrot plants that were only a couple of inches tall. "Be gentle with them."

I told the man that I needed a trowel and a wide-brimmed hat like his. He gestured for me to follow him. I liked how he said that: "Be gentle with them." I wanted to start telling people to be gentle with things. It seemed like a good indicator of kindness—to be able to say that and truly mean it.

He unlocked the tool shed, and we found what we needed inside. With a bucket and trowel in hand, I went to the opposite end of the carrot bed and squatted down in the dirt. The weeds came out easily—the soil was soft and moist—and I found a good working rhythm. A couple of hours must have passed before the man and I finally converged.

I was on my way back to the library when the dinner bell rang. Once again, there was no blackboard and no Uncle Peter, and the colonists seemed much more relaxed and sociable. I got up as everyone was eating to announce that the first day of rehearsals would be that night. Everyone who had signed up—as well as anyone who wanted to join—should come to the dining hall at seven o'clock.

By the time I had finished eating, it was almost seven. I enlisted some help in moving a few of the dining tables, clearing a space which would serve as the stage. Soon everyone had left except for the would-be actors: a group of twenty or so boys and girls (including Claudio, I was glad to see), who seemed to be excited.

"We're all actors," I began. "Every last one of us. We are acting when we pretend to be happy about something that is actually making us sad, or when we pretend to be listening to someone when, in fact, we are not."

I paused to let this sink in. The children looked at me attentively, with only a few exceptions.

"We'll be putting on a play, but before we think too much about that, we're going to do some acting exercises." I grouped the children into threes or fours and told them that I would be giving each group a children's book.

"These are books that most of you have not read," I said. "They are not *Little Red Riding Hood* and *The Three Little Pigs*. Each group will have some time to prepare a short performance of your book, and we will then take turns doing these in front of everyone else. The other groups will try to guess what the book is about, based on your performance. Here's the catch: you can't use words or props. Only actions and facial expressions."

The children buzzed about excitedly in their groups—I was reminded of the students at my acting studio, all of them eager to try being someone new for a change, if only for a few moments.

The first group got up to perform—I did not remember what book I had given them, but it seemed to involve a lot of stomping and chasing each other around. The other children yelled out guesses, and, in the end, the group members (who looked genuinely surprised that nobody had guessed correctly) informed us that it was a book about a cat that gets adopted by a family who has a big and unfriendly dog.

By the time the last group performed, we were all worn out, and I sent the children off with a few tired, congratulatory words. There were things I needed to work on for the escape, but I was exhausted and could hardly muster up the energy to take my clothes off before dropping onto my bed and falling asleep.

# THIRTY-ONE

The next day, Uncle Peter was back. The blackboard period was especially long at lunch, perhaps to make up for all the sins that had happened while he was gone. He was in top form, going from a calm whisper to an incensed roar in mere seconds, pacing back and forth in front of the blackboard. He succeeded in squashing down any elevations in mood that had occurred in his absence. When I went by his office for our interview later, he was in high spirits.

"It's good to be back," he said, gesturing for me to have a seat. "Yes, yes, yes!"

I nodded in agreement.

"I don't know how you did it—living all those years in that garbage dump of a city," he said.

"You were in Santiago?" I asked. I turned on the tape recorder. Uncle Peter frowned.

"I was doing business there."

"Oh?"

"But you and I will talk more about that later," he added, with finality.

"Last time, we left off with you roaming around the German countryside, attracting followers everywhere you went."

"Ah, yes," Uncle Peter said, leaning back in his chair. It was the summertime, and I had a light rucksack with a blanket and a canteen and some food in it. Everywhere I went, I was welcomed with open arms, and everything I asked for I was given. Rides to the next village, a hay-filled barn to spread my blanket, a warm meal at a family's supper table—all these things were given to me by the grace of God, and I began to realize that I had a mission in this world.

"After a while, these followers were begging me to settle down and start a church, a place where they could hear me speak every week and where we could all build a spiritual community under God. I could not start a colony in Germany—land was too expensive, you see— and I heard from a friend that the far-away country of Chile was essentially giving away land. I went to the Chilean consulate and bought a 4,400-acre tract of land, sight unseen. I traveled there with a small group of my followers, and we began to rebuild the decaying ranch that was on the land. Two years after that, the rest of my followers emigrated here—another two hundred of them—officially forming the Colony. That was twenty-six years ago."

"The Colony is built on 4,400 acres of land?" I asked.

"No, no," Uncle Peter said, waving his hand dismissively. "That was the original piece of land. Since then, we've annexed many neighboring acreages—we are now at ten times that: 45,000 acres."

"I noticed there was an old church near the blueberry fields," I said.

Uncle Peter's face contorted for a brief moment and then he coughed violently into his handkerchief.

"The church was sold to us by an order of nuns that was looking to move farther south–to where there are more Mapuche Indians for them to convert—I mean 'help.'"

I decided not to press it, and Uncle Peter launched into a tiresome explanation of how the other lots were acquired. I struggled to pay attention and eventually managed to ask him a series of irrelevant questions that knocked him off track. He noticed the time and declared the interview to be over. I thanked him for his time and stood up.

"One more thing," Uncle Peter said. "You know how to use a typewriter, correct?"

I nodded.

"Good—you are one of the only ones here who does. Therefore, I will require your assistance with a very delicate and important task. A guard will come to get you after dinner. Do exactly as he says."

# THIRTY-TWO

I found the carrot-weeding man elbows-deep in a bush. "Green beans," he explained, jostling his half-filled basket. He told me to grab a basket from the shed. If I wanted to, I could work opposite him, he conceded. I squatted down across the bed from the man and began picking green beans.

"You can pull them harder than that," he said, without looking up. He showed me how to yank the beans off and assured me it would not hurt the plant.

"Thank you," I said. "My name is Javier."

"I know."

I waited for him to volunteer his own name.

"You're Juan, right?" I said. I didn't look up as I said this. That seemed to be the rules of the game when talking in the fields: it's allowed, but no making eye contact or pausing, or you'll get slowed down.

"Victor," he said.

We picked in silence for a while—the beans were the exact same shade of green as the rest of the plant, which made finding them a challenge.

"I work in the kitchen," I said. "Making breakfast in the mornings."

Victor was a couple of paces ahead of me.

"What's your favorite breakfast that we make here?" I said.

The bush in front of Victor shook under his rough, exploring hands. I looked away.

"Sausages and eggs," he said quietly. "My father would make them."

There was something in the corners of his mouth, a slight downturn—subtle enough that I was not sure I had seen it. But then I looked at the rise and fall of his breathing and noticed that it had slowed down a bit. I thought there might be something there with his father, but I didn't want to explore just yet.

"You weren't born here?" I said.

"In Valdivia," he said. "Have you been?"

I shook my head. I knew only that it was an old, wood-shingled city in the south. Victor told me about the city, that it was built at the juncture of two rivers—the Rio Valdivia and the Rio Calle Calle.

I thought about the rivers and about a father who woke up early enough to make breakfast for his son. "Did you fish much, growing up?" I said.

"My father was a fisherman," he said. Again, the corners of his mouth—there it was.

"And my mother," he continued, "a server at one of the restaurants that lined the fisherman's wharf. They met one night at a dance, and out I came ten months later. We were all happy, but, then, when I was twelve, my mother discovered the German Club. There were lots of

Germans—Valdivia was colonized by them in the 1800s as part of Chile's efforts to populate the south.

"At this German Club, my mother gets involved with some young skinheads. You know what that is? And then, one morning, real early, just after my father has gone out to his fishing boat, she wakes me up and pulls me by the hand to the bus station. We're going on an adventure, she tells me, but I want my father to come, too. We catch the first northbound bus of the day, and we're banging at the gates to the Colony that same afternoon."

"I never saw my father again," Victor said, "and he never saw his wife, either."

Neither of us said anything for a few moments. I knew that Victor was someplace else—a remote and vulnerable place.

"Listen," I said, "I need a hat—the sun is getting to me."

Victor looked over at the shed.

"You don't have to come along," I said. "I'd just need to borrow the keys."

Victor hesitated.

"It's all the same to me," I said, shrugging.

He handed me the keys, and I went over to the shed. I knew I didn't have much time; there was only so long it could take to pull a hat from the basket by the door. I found a rope coiled tightly in the corner and tossed it out the back window of the shed. I did the same with a hammer that was dangling from the edge of a bucket. I'd come back to get them later. When I emerged from the shed, Victor was looking my way. I waved and lifted the hat. It was too easy, sometimes.

We picked beans until the dinner bell rang. I walked back to the library slowly, giving Ernesto some time to leave for the dining hall. The library was empty when I finally arrived. I went into the Library Staff Only room and retrieved my tape recorder and a blank cassette. I pressed the Record button down and hurried over to the dining hall. There were only a few stragglers in line—everyone else was sitting and eating—and, by the time I had my tray of food, there were only a few empty seats. These seats were, as usual, all clustered near the front of the room, where Uncle Peter and his tall blackboard stood. I took a seat right up next to Uncle Peter, my tape recorder whirring quietly in the pocket of my pants, its microphone carefully positioned near the opening.

Uncle Peter worked his way through a few of the names on the list.

"Who's next here?" Uncle Peter said, craning his neck to look at the blackboard. "Marta S."

A woman slowly got to her feet.

"It seems to me," Uncle Peter said, "that this is the third time you've been on the blackboard this month."

Marta was shaking her head slowly, back and forth. Uncle Peter looked over at one of the guards and made a gesture with his hand. The guard whipped out a small notebook and began to flip through it, counting silently with a dip of his head. He looked up at Uncle Peter and nodded.

Uncle Peter turned to the rest of us, triumphantly. "It seems like we have a bit of a troublemaker here, wouldn't you say? A pest, even. Are you a pest, Marta S?"

I could see Marta's eyes growing wider, her face growing redder.

"Answer the question!" he demanded.

"I don't know," Marta said. "I don't think I am."

"She doesn't think she is," Uncle Peter said, turning away from her. "Why don't you tell us why your name is on the blackboard, then, and we will decide for ourselves whether you are a pest or not."

Marta S. looked around the room accusingly, looking for a clue as to who had put her name on the board. I could see then that the sinner's blackboard was a brilliant way to breed distrust among the colonists. This lack of group cohesion meant that Uncle Peter did not have to fear an uprising or revolution among his ranks. I looked up at him. His posture was perfect, and his eyes were fixed on Marta S.

"I'm waiting!" Uncle Peter said. "And I *hate* waiting."

"Maybe my name is on there because I was rude to a kitchen worker who asked me to clean off—"

"THAT IS NOT A SIN!" Uncle Peter roared. His voice dropped to barely a whisper. "And you know that very well, you pest."

"Uncle Peter," Marta S. said "I'm begging you—"

"Stop it with your STUPID BLABBERING! Are you going to make me repeat myself? You are nothing but a CLOD OF DIRT!"

I looked up—Uncle Peter's glass eye seemed to be vibrating in its socket. Here was a man who spent much of his time telling people to shut up. I intended to use that to my advantage.

Uncle Peter gestured at the guards, and they advanced on Marta S. with a potato sack in hand. I lowered my head until it was directly over my bowl of soup. There were fat globules floating there and chunks of meat that were tenderly bumping up against potatoes and carrots. I tried to lose myself in the act of eating soup. The meat had once been a cow—I could see it then, grazing contentedly in the field—and the potatoes had once been buried beneath the ground, lifted out triumphantly by rough hands and scrubbed in the kitchen sink not far from where I sat. I continued on in this way, thinking about the carrots, onions, garlic, and parsley, until I got to the barley. I had never seen barley growing anywhere and had no idea what it would look like. Something like wheat, perhaps.

"I'll tell you what I did," Marta S. said quietly.

Uncle Peter held up his hand—the guards stopped advancing.

"I was working in the fields yesterday, and it was so very hot that I almost fainted. I needed to cool off, and I was not far from the river, so I went down there. I didn't want to wet my clothes, so I took them off and jumped into the river and then right back out. Nobody saw me—I didn't think anybody saw me." She looked around accusingly.

"You took your clothes off," Uncle Peter said, "in a place other than your bedroom or the bathroom?"

This did not sound like much of a sin to me.

"I was almost fainting from the heat, Uncle Peter!"

"WHAT IF a group of boys had walked by? WHAT IF a group of men?"

"I was very quick, Uncle Peter. I would have heard them—"

"SILENCE! I'm thinking."

We waited for Uncle Peter to pass his judgment. Marta S. looked fearfully at the guards who were still surrounding her.

"Step back," Uncle Peter called to his guards, waving them away. "We won't be needing the potato sack."

"Oh, thank you, Uncle Peter!" Marta S. said.

Uncle Peter looked around at the rest of us. "Does it feel like this room is hot to you, right now?"

Nobody knew what the right answer was. Marta S. looked at him uncertainly.

"You look warm," Uncle Peter said, turning back to Marta S. "Maybe you'd like to take a swim?"

"I don't—"

"Take your clothes off."

Marta S. looked around. "Uncle Peter . . ."

"NOW!"

Marta S. undid her hair bonnet and let it drop. She fixed her gaze on the floor—her face and neck bright red. She undid the buttons on the front of her dress and lifted it off. She was strong and stocky—the way you'd expect a woman who spends most days in the fields to look. Her underwear was beige and utilitarian, and had been mended many times over.

"The rest of it, too," Uncle Peter said. He had turned off the microphone. The effect was somehow menacing.

Marta S. was crying now, tears streaking down her round cheeks. She unhooked her bra and shrugged it off her shoulders. Then she stepped out of her underwear. Her face and chest were flushed a blotchy red. There were tremors running through her flesh, and I wanted nothing more than to wrap a blanket around this woman and take her as far away from this place as possible.

"There!" Uncle Peter said. "Now for your swim."

He walked over to Marta S., slowly. Then he picked up a bowl of soup from a neighboring table and dumped it over her head. She shrieked—more from surprise, I hoped. I dipped a finger into my own soup to see how hot it was. I was relieved to find it was merely warm by this point.

"I need some help here," Uncle Peter said.

Nobody moved.

"Anyone who doesn't help Marta S. with her swim might enjoy taking a swim WITH HER!"

There was a flurry of movement, and every colonist in the room lurched forward to pour their soup on Marta S. She shut her eyes tightly and held her arms stiffly at her sides. I looked around until I found Claudio. He was staring at his bowl of soup in abject horror, being pulled along by a group of boys. His face was ashen, and he looked like he had taken a turn for the worse since I had last seen him. I tried to catch his eye to reassure him but did not succeed.

I noticed then that many of the colonists were opting to take their water glasses with them—whether they were being kind or had simply run out of soup, I didn't know.

I picked up my water glass and walked over to Marta S. Bits of food were tangled in her hair. I did not know what was said at a baptism. I poured the water gently onto her head.

"God help you," I said under my breath.

# THIRTY-THREE

Uncle Peter announced that Marta S. would be tied to a chair (in her current state of undress) and left to sit outside the dining hall for the next 24 hours. Anyone spotted talking to her or giving her food would join her. After the colonists had filed out of the dining hall, I grabbed a mop and helped the clean-up crew with the daunting task ahead of them. We were almost done when I was approached by a guard. He gestured with his head for me to follow him. I was feeling obstinate and tired of people who tried to get away with not speaking.

"Yes?" I said. I squeezed the mop into the bucket and then slowly swirled it around the pool of liquid at our feet. By not looking at him, I was forcing him to speak.

"Follow me," he said.

"Oh, yes," I said. "I'm supposed to help Uncle Peter with an important and delicate task."

"We need to go this minute."

He followed me closely as I returned the mop to the kitchen.

"We'll be stopping at the library," said the guard. "Uncle Peter has asked that you bring something to write on and your tape recorder."

"Of course."

After a quick stopover in the library, we were back on the road. When we reached the blueberry fields, the guard stopped abruptly. He cursed under his breath.

"What is it?" I asked.

"I forgot," he said. "I was supposed to blindfold you at the library."

I looked around. There was not a person in sight.

"I won't tell Uncle Peter," I said generously.

He looked relieved. Then he reached into his pocket and brought out a thick black strip of cloth. He came up behind me and tied it over my eyes.

"It's a bit tight," I said. It wasn't really—I was just trying to remind him that I was a human, like him. People are less likely to harm someone if they see them as a fellow human. The guard loosened the blindfold.

"Thank you," I said. "I'm Javier, by the way."

"Leonardo," said the guard. "No more talking now."

Then we were on our way again. I tried to keep track of where we were going—32 steps straight, then a sharp right turn and 26 steps, etc.—but it's hard enough to walk while blindfolded, let alone keep track of where one is going. It seemed like we were going around in circles. Perhaps the guard was trying to compensate for having forgotten the blindfold. Finally, we stopped, and I heard the creak of a door being pushed open. Leonardo led me up three large steps and into a building of some sort. I gave a cough, and it echoed well. I thought of the old wooden church I had come across the other day. Leonardo spoke briefly to someone, and then we began a sharp descent down a staircase. When we reached the bottom, Leonardo pulled my blindfold off. I rubbed my eyes and looked around. We were in a concrete bunker, empty except for two hard wooden chairs facing each other in the middle of the room.

"Sit," Leonardo said, pointing at one of the chairs. "Uncle Peter will be here soon." He left the room, closing the door firmly.

I sat and listened. Leonardo seemed to be just outside the door, talking to someone in low whispers. Then there was much shuffling of feet, and the door swung open. Uncle Peter gave me a nod and sat down opposite me.

"We have apprehended a group of men," he began. "They were plotting to assassinate General Augusto Pinochet. I will be questioning these men myself, but I need someone to take down the information they give us—someone who has a tape recorder and can then transcribe the tapes into readable documents."

"Of course."

I didn't want to have anything to do with this "questioning" process, but, now that I was here, I did not think Uncle Peter would let me turn back.

"I'd be happy to help you out."

Uncle Peter got up abruptly. "I will call you into the questioning room when we are ready for you. And a word of warning: some of the men might need to be *encouraged* to speak."

My mouth was dry. I was afraid of how my voice would come out if I tried to say something, so I simply nodded. Uncle Peter left, and, once again, I was alone in the room.

My legs needed to be moving, so I got up and began pacing around the room.

The door swung open, and Leonardo poked his head into the room. "Time to go," he said. He led me down a narrow corridor, stopping just in front of an unmarked door. I stood there, unsure of what to do.

"It's soundproof," Leonardo said. He pointed at a small, latched slot at the base of the door, the kind used to deliver food to those who were inside. It could be opened only from the outside. Then he began a hasty retreat.

"Wait," I said, but he was already halfway down the corridor.

I took three long breaths and tried to think of a mantra that I could repeat to myself. *Yolks and whites* was all I could think of. I knelt down and unlatched the slot and then slid it aside.

"Hello?" I said.

"Well, look at that," I heard Uncle Peter say cheerfully. "Sounds like we have a visitor. COME IN!"

# THIRTY-FOUR

The room was dimly lit and not very large. The walls were covered in egg cartons. There was a hospital bed and a man tied down onto it. He looked like he had not eaten or slept in days—his cheeks drawn back, his eyes glazed over. Next to the bed, there was a large machine, host to all sorts of gauges and levers. A series of wires were leading out from the machine and onto a small leather cap. The cap was on the man's head. The other wires were connected to electrodes on the man's arms, legs, and chest. All except for three of the wires. These led onto what looked like a smaller version of the leather cap.

"Oh, yes," Uncle Peter said, following my gaze, "that machine is called Schnapps."

I turned my head to look at him, but my eyes stayed riveted to the machine.

"Because," Uncle Peter said, "there's nothing like some schnapps to get a man talking!" He laughed heartily at his joke.

"See this one?" he asked, picking up the smaller leather cap. "Can you guess where this one will go?" He raised his eyebrows at the man and shrugged.

"But I'm being quite rude," he said. "I haven't done proper introductions. Javier, meet my new friend, 146."

I looked over at the man and gave him what I hoped was a reassuring look. Uncle Peter began a long sermon about how he wanted 146 to have as easy a time as possible and that he was going to offer him the opportunity to speak before turning to Schnapps for help. 146 fixed his eyes on one of the concrete walls and thoroughly ignored the proceedings.

"This is your last chance," Uncle Peter said, walking over to the machine. He put his hand over one of the levers and looked at 146. Then he pulled the lever down gently, just a fraction of an inch. The lights flickered off and then on again—once, twice, three times. I kept my eyes trained on the machine, watching the gauges flail around, unsuccessfully trying to block out 146's convulsions. Uncle Peter turned the machine off and waited until 146 had settled down.

"That was one single shot of schnapps," he said. "This machine can dish out six shots of schnapps at a time. Do you understand?"

146 closed his eyes. I was sure he was letting his mind wander to some happy memory—maybe a swim in the river with his brother when he was a boy or his first fumbling attempts at making love behind a dilapidated garden shed. Uncle Peter reached over and unbuckled 146's belt. He undid the fly on his pants and pulled until his pants and underwear were halfway down his thighs.

"Now this little thing," he said, holding up the smaller leather cap, "is going to go on that little thing." He looked up at me—the first time since I had come into the room—and then fastened the cap to the man's genitals. 146 began crying—quietly, in as dignified a manner as I could have imagined—and it was then that I looked at him closely and understood he was more a boy than a man. I jumped up from my chair. I walked over to Uncle Peter and tilted my head next to his ear.

"If you leave now, he might talk to me," I said. "He looks like he's ready."

"You are *not* here to tell me what to do!" he whispered furiously. "You are here to take note of his confession—and nothing more."

We were in a church, and I was to listen to a man's confession. I wanted to tell him to recite a few dozen Hail Marys and he would be fine—but I knew there was no amount of praying that would help him at this point. If he refused to confess, he would be tortured and then killed. If, on the other hand, he chose to confess, he would also be killed.

Uncle Peter turned to 146. "Ready or not," he said, putting a hand on the lever. This time, 146's screams were accompanied by the nauseating smell of burning hair and flesh.

146 breathed in deeply through his nose and out through his mouth. Uncle Peter looked at me. He ran his hand down the machine lovingly and put his hand on the lever. "What's that?" he said. "Did someone order three shots?"

"Turn on the tape recorder," 146 said.

"He speaks!" Uncle Peter said.

"Turn it on."

I pressed Record. The machine began its quiet whirring.

"Why don't you start out by telling us your name," Uncle Peter said.

"My name is Lautaro Sánchez, and I was born in Santiago in 1968," he said. "When I was a kid, my father was taken away from me by the Dictator because he had told a friend of his that he thought the Dictator wasn't doing a good job of running the country. Turns out the friend wasn't a friend after all. I never saw my father again, and my mother faded away until there was hardly anything left of her. Someone told me about a meeting I should attend if I wanted to fight the Dictator, and one thing led to another."

"One thing led to another," Uncle Peter repeated, shaking his head.

It was the mention of the Dictator that finally led me to understand that this was the relationship between Uncle Peter and General Pinochet that Julio had been searching for—Uncle Peter tortured General Pinochet's political prisoners to extract information from them, and, in return, he was given license to do anything he wanted at the Colony.

Uncle Peter began asking 146 a long string of rapid-fire questions—names of fellow revolutionaries, meeting places, future plans, etc. I took notes when necessary but mostly relied on the tape recorder. It didn't matter much anyway—I would be making slight alterations to all of the information 146 was divulging. When Uncle Peter seemed satisfied with the answers he had obtained, he asked me to go summon the guards and to ask one of them to walk me back to my room. Several minutes later, blindfolded and being led home by Leonardo, I was stopped in my tracks by a gunshot.

"What was that?" I asked.

"I didn't hear a thing," Leonardo said.

"That gunshot."

"I didn't hear a thing," he repeated.

# THIRTY-FIVE

I woke up the next morning with stomach cramps and a sore jaw. I had not slept much—and the few hours that I did manage to sleep were haunted by nightmares of torture and murder. The second time I awoke from one of these nightmares, I snuck out to retrieve the rope and hammer that I had left outside the garden shed. When I returned, I tried unsuccessfully to salvage another hour or two of sleep. I took a cold shower in hopes that it would wake me up, but all it did was send me into a bout of shivering.

At breakfast, I asked someone to take my spot at the oatmeal—I couldn't bring myself to face too many people just yet—and I went to slice some apples. A boy came into the kitchen.

"Uncle Peter wants to see you," he said. "Follow me."

I got up reluctantly and followed the boy out into the dining hall. Uncle Peter was sitting at a table, tidily sawing away at a sausage link.

"You did good last night," he said. "You'll need to come help out again tonight."

I could feel my stomach clenching. "I have a rehearsal for the play tonight." I did not, but I would gladly schedule one.

"Oh, don't worry about that," Uncle Peter said. "You can just go ahead and reschedule the rehearsal."

I nodded.

"Sit down," he said.

"I need to get back to the kitchen to clean up," I said.

"They'll manage."

I sat down across from him.

"I trust the play is coming along?"

"I think you'll enjoy it," I said.

"Of course. Come by after lunch today, and we'll continue with the interview."

I was starting to get a headache. I returned to the warm safety of the kitchen, where I tried to eat but found I couldn't. I needed some air. I hurried out of the dining hall and almost tripped over Marta S. She was slumped over in her chair, her wrists and ankles tightly bound, her head tilted down to hide her face behind a curtain of hair. She was shivering and sniffling loudly. I couldn't quite understand what would compel a man to do this to someone—there lay the problem with trying to manipulate Uncle Peter. It's hard to figure out what makes a clock tick if you can't open it up and have a look inside.

I continued towards the library. Ernesto was reading a book on the front porch. He glanced up at me and immediately prescribed a nap in the pillowed children's area. We would go on our daily chicken walk when I awoke, he said. I didn't resist—gratefully heading inside, laying out a chain of pillows and falling down onto them.

I awoke to the sound of Ernesto blowing his nose into a handkerchief. He folded it neatly and tucked it into his pocket.

"You're awake," he said brightly.

I groaned and draped an arm over my face to shield out the glaring sunlight.

"You slept for more than an hour. Now it's time to think of those chickens and their need for exercise."

"Just give me a second," I said. I got up slowly, stretching while on the pillows and then again when I was on my feet. I went to the washroom and splashed cold water on my face. I did something I hadn't done since I was young: I cupped a hand under the faucet and ducked my head to drink. Ernesto was waiting for me outside, talking to the chickens as he cleaned out their coop.

"Who wants to go for a walk?" he said. "Which of my ladies wants to go for a lovely little stroll?"

We set out at a slower-than-usual pace. I was still groggy, and Ernesto seemed to be in a pensive mood.

"You were going to tell me the church story," I said. "The real story of how the Colony annexed the church."

Ernesto kept his eyes on his chickens. "There's something you should know about Uncle Peter," he said. "He has a favorite saying: 'Every man has his price.' Well, it turns out the nuns that used to lived in that church did not have their price. They didn't want to sell their land— and Uncle Peter is not one to take 'No' for an answer."

We walked for a little while longer. I wanted Ernesto to continue—I stayed silent and waited. Soon, we reached the fields. A distant figure pushing a wheelbarrow down a path raised a hand in greeting. The sun was behind them, and all I could see was a silhouette. I shielded my eyes from the sun and saw that it was Victor. I waved back.

"This is where the edge of the church land was," Ernesto said. "There were thirty or so nuns that lived here. They had a tidy garden plot and access to the river. They didn't bother anyone—they just kept to themselves and didn't make any trouble. Uncle Peter bought out a farmer on the far side of the church, and he decided that he wanted to buy the church land. But the nuns weren't interested in selling. Their order had lived there for decades, and they hoped to live there for decades more. He offered them lots of money, but they were happy here—this was their home, and they declined his offers."

"He should have tricked them," I said. "Set up some kind of situation to make them want to leave. A faked Anti-Christ or a letter written from some distant locale that desperately needed their help."

Ernesto looked over at me. "I suppose," he said. "Or he could have just let them be. We can't control everything. What he ended up doing was launching a vicious attack on them. He started out by cutting off their water supply and waking them up every night with a series of loud noises and bright lights that he shined into their rooms. When that wasn't enough, he circulated a fake video of the nuns and priests at an orgy."

I stopped walking. One of my chickens looked down and noticed that it was standing in a patch of dry earth. It lowered itself down and shook its feathers.

"Dust baths," Ernesto said. "They do that so they don't get mites."

I scratched the back of my neck.

"The video was horrible," he continued, "but the nuns put their heads down and prayed for him to let them be."

The other chickens all began to take dust baths, too.

"Then Uncle Peter burned their house down," Ernesto said. "And that was the end of that."

I glanced at the church. "Does Uncle Peter use the church for anything these days?"

"Depends on who you ask."

Neither of us said anything for a while. It was mid-morning, and we were standing on the edge of an expansive field. There was a fenced-off area to one side, where a handful of pigs burrowed into the mud. Beside the pigs was a series of beds—some planted, some fallow—and beyond that was the river.

"What were you doing last night?" Ernesto said. We started walking again—back to the library. Faster, this time. "The lights in my room were flickering on and off—the way they do every so often."

I didn't say anything. Ernesto didn't seem to be expecting an answer.

# THIRTY-SIX

The next three days went by in a blur. My brain seemed to shut itself off in the evenings—recording torture testimonies at the church—and, the rest of the time, it was running at a very low level. I spent most of my time in the Library Staff Only room. I wasn't sleeping much at night, and the little sleep I did get was restless and nightmarish. I dreamt of young men trapped in a burning house and nuns being sent into electroshock convulsions. I was grinding my teeth constantly, and my gut was a knot that I struggled unsuccessfully to loosen in the washroom.

The truth was that Uncle Peter frightened me. He was cruel and unpredictable, and seemed to genuinely enjoy inflicting harm on others.

In order to manipulate someone, I would tap away at their protective shell until it cracked open. There were weaker spots that I worked away at—sometimes a vulnerability, sometimes a particular moral grounding— but, in the end, there was always some bit of humanity at the core for me to work with. Uncle Peter was uncrackable. He was inhumane and amoral—and there was also the threat of what would happen if I got caught. There would be no expulsion from the Colony. I would be tortured, surely, and then killed.

I tried to work on the escape, but all I saw were images of Claudio being taken into Uncle Peter's bedroom; of electrodes being adhered to my bare skin; of Elena's face as she realized that I had shown up alone, without her son. I tried to remember why I was doing this, and all I could come up with was my happiness being manipulated at the Santiago International Airport.

I needed Julio and Rodolfo here with me—their calm, their analytical minds, their investigative abilities. Without help, I knew I wouldn't be able to carry out this Manipulation.

On the fourth day, I was late for breakfast. I didn't sleep in—I just didn't care anymore. Anita was nowhere to be found, so I began helping a colonist core and slice apples. He was a young man, and he was working away at the apples slowly and meticulously.

"If you wouldn't mind," he said, after a few minutes, "we are to be slicing them far thinner than that. Paper thin, just so you can see some light shining through."

I stopped in mid-slice and turned my head to glare at him. "Listen up," I said through gritted teeth, "I am sick and tired of people telling me what to do—I will slice these goddamn apples however thick I want to—got it?"

My voice had gotten louder and louder, and, by the end, everyone else in the kitchen was staring at me silently.

"What are you looking at?" I called out. "Get back to work!"

I felt someone take ahold of my arm. It was Anita. "I need your help," she said.

I was shaking.

"Would you wash the dining-hall tables?" Anita asked.

I nodded and went to find a bucket and rags. The slippery feel of the warm, bleachy water, the circular motions—neither did much to calm me down. The sun rose over the Cordillera, and it glared off the tables. Anita came into the dining hall and pulled a rag out from where it was tucked into her apron. She swished it around in the bucket of water and gently twisted it. We washed adjacent tables, and then she turned to me.

"You doing okay?" she said.

"Fantastic," I said.

Anita dropped her rag into the bucket and walked over. She opened her arms and pulled me into a hug. Her body was a nest of pillows that I let myself fall into. I cried like I hadn't since I was a child—long, heaving sobs that seemed to pull at every corner of my body. Anita rubbed my back and didn't say a word.

"You're not having an easy time here," she said, finally.

"I'm not," I said, my eyes shut tightly. I was finished—I no longer had to put on a face, to part my hair on the other side, to look for subtle changes in body language.

"You're better than him," Anita said.

I shook my head. He was better—he had outcompeted me. His Manipulations were far superior, and he didn't have a shred of humanity for me to work with.

"You're not alone here," Anita said.

She was right, of course. I thought of Ernesto and Claudio. Of Julio and Rodolfo, who were not here but who had given me tools to work with. Of Elena. I lifted my head up from Anita's shoulder—I felt buoyed.

"Go on, now," she said, shooing me away with her rag. I had not hugged my own mother since I was a young boy—she had died giving birth to my sister María Paz.

We wiped down tables side by side for a few minutes, neither of us saying anything.

"How did you end up here?" I asked. I wasn't trying to gain anything by asking her this—I was genuinely interested.

Anita held up a finger and then walked over to the window and peeked out. "I lived in the town just outside here. There used to be an order of nuns on this property— my job was to come over every day and make lunch for them. When the order dissolved and the nuns left, I decided I would open a restaurant. Nothing fancy, just a little place. It had been my dream since I was a little girl. I had hardly begun planning when a group of men with guns came to my house one night and marched me over to the Colony. I remember the feeling when I was walking through that gate—that feeling of not knowing if I would ever come back out. The men took me to a room, where I met Uncle Peter for the first time. I had heard much about him but had never seen him. He told me that he had acquired the land that the nuns lived in and, therefore, had acquired my services as well. I tried to tell him that I had plans to start my own restaurant, but he said that this would be my own restaurant. And since everyone who worked at the Colony needed to live there, the men would go to my house and bring a few bags of things. I begged him to let me go back to town, but he wouldn't budge."

I tried to process the story Anita had just told me. "Why?" I said.

"The nuns," Anita said. "I knew too much about what had happened with the nuns, and Uncle Peter didn't want anyone to find out."

Before I could ask about the nuns, a man rushed into the dining room to let us know that there was smoke coming from the oven. Anita left, and I hurriedly finished wiping down the tables.

While breakfast was being served, Uncle Peter announced that he would be leaving on a trip for a couple of days. I was relieved—there hadn't been a play rehearsal in a while, and I had begun to worry about Claudio. Uncle Peter seemed excited with his own announcement—I was afraid that he would be returning with a new cohort of political prisoners. I asked Uncle Peter if I might make an announcement. I went up to the microphone and tried to muster up the energy to promise an exciting play rehearsal that very night.

"Tonight, we'll be figuring out who will play which role," I said—which seemed like a good way to get a good turnout.

When I left the kitchen that day, I was in higher spirits than I had been in in days. There was work to be done at the library—Ernesto was trying to figure out what to do about some mouse droppings that he had found, and there was a group of boys arriving any minute for a story time.

"No chicken walk today," Ernesto said.

"You need some help?"

"I need a cat," he said. "A library cat to keep the mice away."

I went outside to greet the chickens and to get out of the library. The sun was tucked behind a cloud, but it was warm out. A few minutes passed, and I heard Ernesto call out my name. I hurried back inside.

"We have a situation," he said, pulling me into the children's section.

There were a group of boys sitting on the ground—one of them was sitting all by himself, an ocean of pillows and carpet separating him from the others. He was folded up into a tiny package, his head in his arms, his shoulders heaving.

"I had just started telling the kids a story," Ernesto whispered, "but then they all started yelling and moved away from that one boy, who won't stop crying. I think he peed his pants."

I looked around the room.

"Their supervisor just left them here and took off," Ernesto said.

I went over to the boy and squatted down next to him.

"Want to see some chickens?" I said.

He shook his head.

"There are some chickens out back—we can go pet them and look for eggs."

He seemed to be considering it. Ernesto relaunched his story—I gently pulled the boy by his arms until he was standing and then led him out into the garden. We went into the chicken coop and sat down on a grassy patch. I gave him a handful of grain and showed him how to lay his hand flat on the ground so that the chickens would peck at it.

"It's not fair," he said quietly. "That one's not letting the others get any."

He was right—I picked up the hen that was at the very top of the pecking order and held her in my lap. The other chickens gratefully pecked at the food. We talked about the chickens, and I told him that I was new to the Colony, having just arrived from Santiago. His name was Pedro—like Claudio, he lived in Santiago and was a student in the Intensive Boarding School program. Things had been fun at first, and the other boys were nice. There was a lot of playing soccer, which he loved, and the food was better than anything his father cooked. Then he had been made Sprinter, and that had been okay, too. Running from one end of the Colony to the other was fun, and he got to deliver important messages from Uncle Peter to the Colonists.

"But last night," Pedro said, "a guard came during my prayer time and took me to Uncle Peter's room. Uncle Peter gave me something to drink—it tasted terrible— and then I was dizzy, and he said that, when you're dizzy, you should have a bath. . . ."

Pedro began to cry. I felt like I might be sick. I dug my fingernails into the dirt until it was painful and put my arm around his shoulders. He flinched—of course, the last thing he needed was to have another grown man touching him. I had no idea whatsoever how to comfort a boy in a situation like this—saying "it's okay" would be dishonest; saying "don't cry" would be ridiculous. If there was ever a reason to cry, this was it.

"Now it hurts me," Pedro said, sniffling, "down there."

I heard a noise and looked up at the library. Ernesto was standing there.

"I'm going to get you some pants," I said to Pedro.

I told Ernesto about the situation while we rummaged through the lost-and-found. He told me that one of the nurses at the clinic was known to be particularly sympathetic towards these kinds of things. I found a pair of pants and took them out to Pedro.

"Put these on," I said, turning my back to give him some semblance of privacy. I told him we were going to go see a nurse who would help him out. We walked to the clinic at a quick clip. Fortunately, we avoided running into any of his friends or any guards. I found the office of the sympathetic nurse and knocked on the door. A young woman opened the door—she took one look at Pedro's tear-streaked face and gave me a heartbroken look.

"He's a Sprinter," I whispered to the nurse. She gestured with a wave that no more explanation was needed. I said goodbye to Pedro and let myself out of the clinic. The lunch bell rang, and I let myself be carried towards the dining hall in a wave of colonists.

# THIRTY-SEVEN

I had just started eating when the speakers buzzed on and Uncle Peter's voice boomed across the dining hall.

"My dear colonists," he said. "I am a happy man today. I am proud, too—proud to announce that, in just a few short days, we will be bestowing three new boys with the honor of becoming Sprinters!"

The colonists clapped.

"And who are these lucky boys?" Uncle Peter was pacing rapidly, his gestures brimming with excitement. "Alejandro Gonzalez!" he called out, pointing at a boy sitting not far from me. "Lalo Mittenberg!"

The colonists turned to look at another young boy.

"And, last, but not least, one of our newest boys, Claudio Soto!"

I followed Uncle Peter's gaze until I found Claudio. His ears were red, and he was looking down at his plate with fierce concentration.

"On Sunday evening, after dinner," said Uncle Peter, "these boys will receive their new titles and begin serving as Sprinters immediately thereafter."

That night, once the dining-hall tables had been shoved to one side of the room, we had our second official rehearsal. The children were in high spirits, and I led them through a series of acting exercises. I asked someone to help me gather some chairs, and, after a pointed stare, Claudio raised his hand. When we were far enough away from the group, I asked how he was doing.

"When can I go home?" he said, his voice hardly more than a whisper. His face was pale, and his eyes narrow and darting.

"Very soon," I said. I couldn't risk giving him any actual details. "You'll have to be ready to leave with just a moment's notice."

He nodded his head. "But on Sunday, he said today at lunch—I don't *want* to be a Sprinter!" His voice was getting louder, and I looked around at the rest of the children.

"I know," I whispered, squatting down next to him. "But we need to pick the right time. I have a plan. I'm going to need your help on the day of the escape."

Claudio looked at me, wide-eyed and serious. "I can help—I can do anything I need to do. What do I need to do?"

"It's very simple," I said. "You're going to need to act."

We returned to the dining hall and set the chairs down off to the side. I gathered everyone around me and began assigning roles.

"In Act One, you're Uncle Peter," I said. "You three are farmers; you're a sheep; you two are a horse . . ."

By the time I was done, everyone had several roles—most of the children had six or seven. We worked through the play in rough motions—they did not have scripts, so I just ran them through the general movements and stage entrances and exits. Then I waved the children in until they formed a tight semi-circle.

"Listen carefully," I said. "This play is going to be the most exciting thing to ever happen at the Colony—but only if we are able to keep everything about it a secret. Don't tell anyone anything about it, or it'll spoil the surprise."

The children nodded their heads (they were mirroring my own nodding head). A chain of yawns swept through them, and I herded them out the door.

# THIRTY-EIGHT

I awoke the next morning feeling restless. I hurried into my regular clothes—pants, suspenders, white shirt—and made my way down to the river. I listened sharply for birds, but there was only silence.

I tromped through the tall grasses of the riverbank, and water began seeping through the seams of my shoes. The sun was just coming up, and, as it filtered through the water, I could see the ghostly outlines of fish. I knew nothing whatsoever about fish, but I knew then with complete certainty that, when this whole thing was over, I would be one of those men who wakes up while it's dark out and goes fishing in the early hours. I had known things with this level of certainty before—that I would be a father by the time I was thirty; that I would walk across the mountains, from Chile to Argentina—things that had never worked out. But, somehow, this time, it felt different.

I wandered around for a few moments, hoping to catch a glance of a deer or other woodland creature. I was anxious to be warmed by full sunlight—rather than the canopy-filtered one—and it was probably time for me to report to the kitchen. The walk back went by quicker than I would have liked.

I spent the next hour or so hard at work—scrubbing, peeling, chopping—and went out to serve the oatmeal when the breakfast bell rang. When we had all finished eating our breakfasts, I made my way over to the library. Ernesto was doing some library-related task that I did not bother asking him to explain.

"Chicken time?" I said.

We set out with our worm-sticks and our eagerly trailing poultry.

"I want to go visit Angela today," Ernesto said.

I stopped walking. "Keep walking," he said.

We walked past the fields and towards a small hill. We wound our way down a row of headstones, and then Ernesto stopped in front of one. There were two adjacent plots. One of them had Angela's name on it and the years of her birth and death. And below it, the phrase "*Our ship . . .*"

"What does that mean, 'our ship'?"

"That one's for me," Ernesto said, ignoring my question, as he pointed at the space next to Angela's grave. He dangled his worm stick over it, and the chickens began scratching at the plot. We were quiet for several minutes. Ernesto brushed some dirt off Angela's headstone.

"I was married when I was still in high school," I said. "It was our graduation day, and, instead of going to the ceremony, we went to City Hall and got married. We were eighteen years old, and we'd been in love since we were fourteen. We moved in together, into her parents' house—they had a large basement—and I was as happy as could be. Then, one weekend she went with her parents to the beach. I couldn't get the time off work, so I didn't go."

I could feel Ernesto tense up.

"They were hit by a truck on their way home," I said quickly. "She wasn't wearing a seatbelt."

I was having trouble swallowing.

"I'm so sorry," Ernesto said.

My wife's headstone was even simpler than Angela's. Just her name, the dates, no phrase below it. I knew nothing of what she wanted done in case of death—we were far too young to ever think that it was a possibility. I kept it together at the funeral up until the first shovelful of dirt was tossed onto the casket. That sound—the hollow tumbling of soil hitting wood—reeled up a bucket of grief from a well that I had left unprotected, and my father pulled my heaving shoulders into his chest.

I tried to continue living in the basement of her parents' house, but I could hardly look at them without one of us breaking into tears, and so I moved home. I stayed in my bedroom for several weeks. I took my meals there and read a little bit, but, mostly, I just lay on my bed and looked up at the ceiling and thought about her. I told my father that I would not see any visitors, and the phone rang and rang until my friends stopped trying.

There was something about being a widow at eighteen that felt grossly unfair. My father and I never discussed it much—that we had each lost our wives at a young age—not until I was in my late twenties and he was dying of pancreatic cancer. It was only then that I would sit on his hospital bed for hours at a time, and we would lay our stories out carefully between us like two old men playing cards.

"I want to let her go," I said, "but I can't."

Ernesto looked surprised. "Why would you want to let her go? There's lots of room in there. In any case, it's not that easy."

I must have had a look on my face, because he put his hand on my arm. There was a tenderness to the gesture that I hadn't expected. "Keep her there," he said. "It doesn't mean you won't meet someone else or get married again. It just means that you're giving her a place to stay, someplace warm and protected."

I had been putting on a performance for myself—acting for all these years as if I wanted to let her go, when, in fact, I wanted her to stay. I felt something in me release—there was an unclenching somewhere inaccessible.

"I want to tell you something," I said to Ernesto, once we were back in the library, "but you need to keep it to yourself."

"Let's hear it."

"There are boys here from Santiago for boarding school. There's one who is going to be made a Sprinter this Sunday. One of the boys—his mother hired me to get him out of here."

Ernesto raised his eyebrows. "You're not a reporter."

I ran my hand along the top of a bookcase. "I haven't been entirely honest," I said. "Not with you, not with anyone." I was thinking of the Manipulations I had been running for years—always playing this part or that, always trying to get something from someone. Julio had told me to find someone I could trust, and I realized that, without him or Rodolfo, I would need help.

"I'm working on a plan," I said, "but it still needs some work."

Ernesto nodded seriously.

"And I need your help," I said.

Most of the colonists were already sitting at tables when we arrived at the dining hall for lunch.

"A short announcement!" I called out.

The colonists slowly turned their heads in my direction.

"We'll be putting on our play next week, and I still need people to help out with costumes and with the set."

There were some whispers and nods.

"Come see me," I said.

By the time I had piled my tray with food and made my way over to an empty seat, there were already a few interested colonists hovering around me. I spent the rest of the meal assessing skills and assigning jobs. I spotted Greta walking by with an empty tray, and I asked my eager volunteers to give me a moment.

"Greta!" I said, getting up. She pretended not to hear me and kept walking. I caught up with her as she was leaving the dining hall.

"The colonists have been talking to me about your orchestra—they want you to be a part of the play."

"I am too busy," she said.

"It would be a gift to everyone to have your music there."

Greta shrugged.

I needed to try something else. "Uncle Peter wants you to do the music for the play."

"Which is the music he want?"

"We're going to need some upbeat German folk music," I said, "and something sad and dramatic. And some music that would work for funny scenes."

"I can do," she said, sighing.

I wanted to say something nice but could think of nothing. "You're giving these children something special by teaching them to play music," I said, finally.

Greta nodded. Her face softened a bit, and she said, "They are getting better. Very slowly, but better."

When I returned to the library, I found Ernesto telling a story to a group of young boys. I stood at the back and listened for a bit. It was about a village in which there was a monster that ate some little boys but not others. He would snatch the children from their bedrooms at night—some of them he would gobble up, and others he would simply return to their beds unharmed. The villagers had a big meeting to try to figure out why he ate some and not others. Perhaps the monster didn't like boys who ate sugar? But no, then he ate little Robin, whose parents did not allow a single grain of sugar to enter his mouth. Perhaps the monster didn't like boys who disobeyed their parents? But no, then he ate Nigel. Those who obeyed their parents? Nope, he soon gobbled up obedient little Elsworth. The parents began to fight amongst themselves—wondering why their boys were eaten while their neighbours' boys were spared, and so on.

The monster continued to terrorize the village until one day, when the smallest boy finally figured it out. He got up in front of all the villagers and told them that there was no rhyme or reason to who the monster ate. He only made it seem like there was so the villagers would be so busy fighting amongst themselves that they would forget about fighting the monster. The monster had tricked the villagers into trying to figure out what they were doing wrong. "We're doing nothing wrong!" cried the smallest boy. "And that monster has got to go!" The next morning, the villagers tracked down the monster and tried giving him a big hug—maybe he needed love! Nothing happened. Then they carried him up to a fiery volcano and tossed him in—that worked much better. The End.

Everyone cheered. I went into the Library Staff Only room and locked the door. I found a blank cassette tape and wrote "ANGRY REBUTTAL TO ANY COMMENT." Then I put it into one of the tape decks. A tape containing one of my interviews with Uncle Peter went into the other. I went through it until I found words and phrases that would serve my purposes, then recorded those onto the blank cassette tape. It was tedious and repetitive work, requiring lots of rewinding and re-playing.

# THIRTY-NINE

The dinner bell rang, and Ernesto yelled for me to take a break. We walked over to the hall together and had not yet entered the building when Ernesto said, "He's back."

I stopped walking. There was something about the tone of the muted voices leaking out the door that did, in fact, indicate a subtle change in mood from the past few meals, when Uncle Peter had been gone.

Sure enough, there he was—standing at the front of the room, microphone in hand. I got into the line and tried to hide behind Ernesto. A colonist who was standing behind me tapped me on the back. I half-turned my head and raised my eyebrows. The colonist pointed at the stage, where Uncle Peter was smiling and signaling for me to come talk to him. I gestured at the lineup, but he shook his head and continued to signal.

"We've got a long night ahead of us," he said, putting an arm around me. "Make sure you eat a big dinner and have a few cups of coffee."

I got back in line and filled my bowl with *porotos granados*, the first traditionally Chilean dish I had eaten since arriving at the Colony, and one of my father's favorites. He would make it at least every other week, often letting me stand on a chair by the stove and gently stir the bubbling stew of beans, squash, and corn. We would eat it with *ensalada a la Chilena*, an invigorating salad of paper-thin slices of raw white onion and tomato wedges. There was no such salad with this meal—though the kitchen had prepared a limp lettuce salad that I doctored with a generous splash of vinegar. I took a seat and let my head hover above the steaming bowl of stew. I needed to cook more when I returned home. More cooking, more fishing, more gardening. I soon found myself in the middle of an especially pleasant daydream (Elena and I hard at work in our garden, harvesting vegetables for dinner while Claudio entertains us on his clarinet) but was pulled out of it abruptly by a burst of microphone feedback.

I felt someone shaking my shoulder and looked up. There was a guard standing over me—Leonardo, from the other night.

"It's time to go," he said. The room was mostly empty, and a woman who must have belonged to the evening kitchen crew had already begun wiping down the tables while another swept the floor. Ernesto was patiently sitting beside me, worrying away at a bump on the bench with his fingernail. Then the lights flickered on and off—one, two, three times—and my heart sank. I followed Leonardo out of the dining hall. We went by the library to pick up the tape recorder and a notepad, and, once we were outside, Leonardo pulled a blindfold out from his pocket.

"It's alright," I said. "I know where we're going."

Leonardo looked down at the ground. "I'll get in trouble if I don't," he said.

I let him put the blindfold on me, and I grabbed onto his arm the way I had seen blind people do. Leonardo fended off my attempts at starting a conversation, and we continued on in silence. We entered what I knew was the church, and I felt the space around me constrict.

"Are you a religious man, Leonardo?"

"We're here," he said. "Just down these steps, and then you can take off the blindfold."

Leonardo led me to the interrogation room and removed my blindfold. I opened the slot at the bottom of the door and announced my presence. There was silence from within, and then the door swung open. Uncle Peter's hair was sprouting every which way, and he could hardly keep still.

"Come in, come in," he said, pulling me into the room. "You've been missing out on all the fun."

I looked over at the bed. There was a man lying there, strapped down tightly. I glanced at Uncle Peter and then back at the man. It was Tibor.

# FORTY

Tibor's eyes were glazed over. His arms were littered with burn marks, and the rising and falling of his chest was erratic and shallow.

"Who is this man?" I said loudly, not taking my eyes off Tibor. There was a danger here—that, in his current state, he might not realize that I needed him to pretend not to know me.

"This man," Uncle Peter said. "No, not this 'man.' This is not a man, this is a Jew."

Tibor looked up at me. "You," he said, his voice weak.

I looked at Uncle Peter—he was busy fiddling with the straps on Tibor's legs. I shook my head at Tibor, ever so slightly, and opened my eyes wide in warning.

Uncle Peter walked over to the machine and put his arm around it. "Me and Schnapps here have been having a lot of fun," he said. I couldn't look at him, nor could I look at Tibor anymore.

"He killed a Nazi," Uncle Peter said, raising his voice. "This creature, this Jew,"—he spat the word out—"has killed one of my own!"

I nodded.

"He's already admitted to killing the man—Dr. Koehler," Uncle Peter said, "but he claims to have acted alone. He won't tell me who helped him—I'm going to find out who it was and make him pay."

I approached Uncle Peter. "He looks like he's barely hanging on," I whispered.

Uncle Peter walked over to the bed and grabbed Tibor's face.

"I have a scalpel," he said. "This is an interesting fact: when I was a child, I wanted to be a doctor. I wanted to see what a lung looked like. A heart."

Tibor looked up, his eyes suddenly clear. "Sure," he said. "A doctor. You already know what I do to doctors."

Uncle Peter yelled something in German and slapped Tibor.

The room was quiet then, and I thought very hard for a few moments. Then I spoke up, not sure what I was going to say until I said it. "I don't know much about Jews," I said, "but I do know this: they hate Nazis—and a man like this one, you've got to think about how much he's hated them ever since he was a child. How he hated nothing more than having to walk around his village with a yellow star on his—"

"Get on with it, already!" Uncle Peter yelled. His mouth twitched violently, and I knew I would have to be better than him.

"What I'm thinking here," I said, hurriedly, "is whether there's something we could do that would be far worse than playing doctor."

He gestured impatiently for me to get on with it.

"I've learned something important from you," I said. "That emotional torture can be more painful than physical torture. What if we postpone this Schnapps business for just a bit, we take him out to the barn tomorrow—the goat barn, it's got that electric fencing—and put him in there to live with the animals. We'll sew a star on his jacket, bring back some memories."

"The goat barn," Uncle Peter said, slowly.

"He'll be ready to talk to you after that," I said. "And we would be reminding the other colonists that they are very fortunate."

Uncle Peter hooked his finger around one of the levers on Schnapps. He tilted his head back in thought. "A few days of living with the animals," he said, "on his hands and knees."

I looked at Tibor. He sagged against the bed, his eyes opened wide, waiting for yet another man to decide for him—go this way and you die, go that way and you live.

# FORTY-ONE

I awoke earlier than necessary and headed off to the barn. The guard on duty confirmed that they had received a new animal this morning. I asked if I could see the new animal, and the guard gestured over to the open-air barn. Tibor was sitting on a bale of hay in a corner. The rest of the barn was home to a dozen or so goats.

"Am I safe from him?" I asked the guard.

"He's not chained to anything," said the guard, "but there's high-voltage electrified fencing around the entire barn. He can be anywhere inside the barn, but he can't leave the structure itself."

"Good," I said. "Though I have to say, he doesn't look very dangerous at all. I'm a bit disappointed."

"That's how Jews are," said the guard. "Uncle Peter said so when he dropped him off last night."

"Well, I won't keep you," I said. "I just wanted to watch him for a bit."

The guard told me I could take as much time as I wanted. Colonists were encouraged to come see Tibor, after all. After he had walked away, I took a step closer to the fence and looked at Tibor. He had been studiously ignoring the conversation, but now he turned to look at me.

"I wouldn't get too close to that fence if I were you," he said. "It's not a pleasant experience."

"Are you okay?"

Tibor shrugged. "There's no Schnapps here."

"Do you have food and water?"

Tibor unhooked a tin cup from a nail on the wall. He walked over to one of the goats and squatted down beside her. He stroked her head gently and then squeezed her teat so that a stream of milk shot into the cup. After a minute or so of this, he tipped the cup back and drank the milk. He stood up and wiped his mouth with the back of his hand.

"Food and water," he said, "all at the same time."

"Just hold on for a few days," I said.

Tibor nodded.

"I have to go make breakfast," I said. "I'll be back soon."

Tibor patted the goat on her head. He reminded me that he had grown up a goatherd and knew how to live amongst them.

The kitchen was a flurry of activity. Anita was nowhere to be found, so I asked a woman who was chopping potatoes if she needed any help. She pushed a pile of potatoes my way and gratefully accepted. When we were done, I left to find someone else who looked like they might need help, and I continued on in this way until the breakfast bell rang.

"I have a very exciting announcement, my dear children!"

Uncle Peter was looking positively radiant—his cheeks ruddy and a smile pasted on his face. He passed the microphone from one hand to the other, waiting for the colonists to be silent.

"I was in Santiago yesterday," he began, his voice dropping down to a whisper, "hunting down a killer."

The colonists leaned forward, anticipating a good story.

"Some time ago, my dear old friend Dr. Koehler fell ill. He was taken to a hospital, where he slowly began to recover his health. One night, a man sneaked into his room and gave him an injection that would take his life. He injected Dr. Koehler, STRAIGHT INTO HIS HEART, with nothing other than a syringe full of GASOLINE!"

The colonists gasped and put their hands to their mouths.

"Through the help of some trusted friends, I was able to find him in Santiago and capture him. AND NOW, my friends, I have brought him to here to the Colony, where he will be living in the goat barn, with HIS FELLOW ANIMALS!

"There is another thing you should know about this animal, and this should come as no surprise to any of you. He is a Jew–a dirty, rotten Jew, and that is why he will be living with the goats, LIKE THE ANIMAL THAT HE IS!"

Uncle Peter invited the colonists to go visit Tibor at any time they liked. He told them that Tibor would be wearing a yellow star on his coat—like all Jews were forced to do during the Holocaust—and that reminding him of this would be a good way to punish him for the unspeakable crimes he had committed.

I retreated into the kitchen to eat a bowl of oatmeal, but I was not very hungry and could eat only a few spoonfuls. Ernesto was waiting for me on the front porch of the library. "We'll go for a short walk without the chickens," Ernesto said, "and then we'll come back and take them out."

We could hear the yelling before we could even see the barn. There was a large crowd of colonists standing around the goat barn. Ernesto and I found a bench to stand on, from which we could see over the shoulders of the crowd. Tibor was leaning up against one of the walls, while a goat rubbed her head against his leg. I scanned the crowd, and found Claudio standing with a group of boys. His expression was vacant—like many of Uncle Peter's torture victims.

"Make him crawl!" yelled one of the colonists.

The guard who was on duty pointed his gun at Tibor. "You heard the man," he called out. "We want to see you on all fours, like the animal that you are."

Tibor dutifully got down on all fours and crawled around the mucky barn floor.

"We want to see him drink the milk!" said another colonist.

I refrained from looking around to see who had spoken. It would do me no good.

The guard gestured at Tibor with his gun. "Do it."

Tibor retrieved his tin cup and made his way over to one of the lactating goats. He reached out and grabbed ahold of her teat.

"The way animals do it," said the guard, loudly. "With your mouth."

Tibor looked up at the man with sudden murderous rage. Then he clamped his lips around the goat's teat and suckled. It seemed then to be the most humiliating act that one human could demand of another.

The colonists' reaction was deafening. There was jeering and shouting. Someone threw an apple into the barn, and it hit Tibor on the back. The vastness of any given person's capacity for violence and hatred is a sad thing. I tried not to blame any of the colonists—they had been bombarded with fear and anger, and then prevented from retaliating against the man who was responsible for generating these emotions. Tibor's presence gave the colonists an opportunity to expel some of these feelings, and they were doing so.

I looked over at Claudio. His fists were clenched, and his little chest was heaving. His eyes landed on mine, and he took a step towards me. I knew then there was going to be some trouble. The colonists were still yelling, and Claudio pushed his way through them, moving towards me desperately.

"I don't want to be here," he said.

I glanced around to see if anyone was paying attention to us. I put a hand on Claudio's shoulder and quietly said, "Be patient—I'm working on it, son. What's important for now, though, is for us to not be seen together."

He screwed up his face. "I DON'T WANT TO BE HERE!" he screamed.

Those who were nearby turned to look at us. I needed to do something, fast. I put my hands on Claudio's chest and pushed him hard enough so that he fell down.

"Get this nuisance away from me!" I said loudly.

At that moment, there was a yell from one of the colonists. Several of the goats were bleating fiercely, and one of them charged at the crowd. It crashed into the electrified fence, rattling it hard and letting out a painful squeal. The guard told the colonists to disperse—if there was any damage to the fence, everyone was going to be in trouble. Claudio had stood up, and I signaled with my hands for him to take it easy. "Easy does it," I whispered. Two boys came by and pulled Claudio away—their group was leaving.

Ernesto and I left along with the rest of the colonists—we did not want to attract any attention to ourselves. The chickens were waiting for us impatiently, clucking and scratching at the ground and looking around.

"Okay, okay," Ernesto said. "Everybody settle down."

We armed ourselves with our worm sticks and headed out into the road in a cloud of dust and cackling.

"That boy back there," Ernesto said.

I nodded, "That's the one. And the goat man—he's coming, too."

Ernesto raised his eyebrows.

"And you?" I said.

Ernesto shook his head. "Oh, no," he said. "I like my library and my storytelling and my scheduled meal times. If I were a younger man, I might take you up on your offer, but I'm too old to start a new life."

We walked in silence for a bit.

"If you're not a reporter," Ernesto said, "then what exactly are you?"

"It was the 1970s," I said, "and General Pinochet had just taken power. I was one of many university students who were unhappy with the direction the country was taking."

I told him about the Faculty wine and cheese, where I'd stumbled into a discussion on Social Psychology and emerged with the kernel of an idea. This was followed by many late nights at the library paging through scientific journals. One of the papers that was referenced most widely turned out to have been written by a graduate student at my university. I tracked him down—he was completing his PhD in Sociology and teaching a couple of courses. Julio was less of an outraged idealist than I was, but he was interested in seeing his theories applied in a real-world context. We worked together to organize a series of Manipulations against the dictatorship. On one occasion, we obtained Pinochet's direct phone number from a seduced secretary and impersonated several foreign heads of state, all of whom urged Pinochet to step down from power. Another time, we applied Julio's theories of group dynamics to convert a peaceful protest into a violent one—we managed to tear down much of the fence around Pinochet's home before the water cannons came. Our attempts were generally unsuccessful–but we learned invaluable lessons that guided future Manipulations.

"So you've got a plan," he said.

"We leave on Sunday," I said. "The day of the big play."

"You've stolen a gun from a guard? A knife?"

"I have a rope," I said. "And a hammer."

Ernesto shook his head. "Nobody leaves the Colony— not unless Uncle Peter says so."

"Then we'll have to get him to say so," I said.

The chickens clucked along contently.

"Do you know about the last time Uncle Peter lost at anything?" Ernesto said.

I shook my head.

"When he and my wife were kids," Ernesto said, his voice dropping down to a more ominous tenor, "they liked to race each other. Angela was slightly faster than him and won every race by a small margin. One morning, Uncle Peter woke up and decided that he would go over to Angela's that day after school and that he would finally outrun her. He ate a large breakfast and tied his shoes as tight as he possibly could, in hopes that this would give him an extra advantage. All day at school, he was bursting with energy, sitting on the edge of his seat and jittering his legs, and, when the bell finally rang, he and Angela hurried home to her house. They lined up at the fallen rake that served as a starting and finishing line, and counted down from three. They raced around the cornfield, once, and Angela beat him handily. 'Again,' Uncle Peter said, and again Angela reached the rake before he did. They raced five or six more times, and, each time, Uncle Peter lost. Finally, he collapsed in a fit of exhaustion and frustration.

"Angela walked him back to his house, and his mother poked her head out and invited them in for a snack. 'Take your shoes off,' his mother said, and Angela slipped off her shoes and padded into the kitchen. 'There's cookies!' she called to Uncle Peter, happily. Uncle Peter was sitting on the ground at that moment, discovering that he could not untie his shoelaces because he had tied them too tightly. With a mouthful of crumbs, Angela came to see what was the matter, and she offered to give it a try. Uncle Peter batted her hands away and told her to go into the kitchen and grab him a fork. Angela obliged, and, when she returned, Uncle Peter snatched the fork from her and began digging it into the knotted laces and pulling on it as hard as he could. He tried and tried, and, then, all of a sudden, the fork slipped out, and he jammed it with all his force right into his eye."

I instinctively raised a hand to cover my eyes.

"Angela says he pulled it out instantly, and it came out with the eyeball on it—but she was just a child at the time."

There was not much to say after that, so we continued our walk in silence. I thought about Uncle Peter's savage competitiveness—the nuns, now this—and it seemed like something I would very likely be able to use against him.

There was much to do before Sunday rolled around. When we returned to the library, I went into the Library Staff Only room to work on the play. The lunch bell rang, and Ernesto and I made our way over to the dining hall. The blackboard was full of names, and I asked Uncle Peter if I could make an announcement before he began.

"The play will be this coming Sunday!" I said. "We will be having a rehearsal tomorrow night and a dress rehearsal on Saturday night."

There was a clatter of protest from the set and costume volunteers. They approached me when lunch was over, clamoring for more time. I apologized for the short deadline and told them that the colonists would enjoy the play regardless and that this was about the children, after all. One of the costume designers shook her head at me. "Without a good costume, you have nothing!"

I didn't use costumes much for my Manipulations—last time I did was in the early years of General Pinochet's dictatorship. It began like most of them did: with a woman walking into my office.

# FORTY-TWO

She was the mistress of a recently exiled man—let's call him Señor Reyes—who happened to be a very famous leftist writer. General Pinochet had assumed power not long before, and he had exiled Señor Reyes to Europe. Unbeknownst to anyone, Señor Reyes had made his way down to Argentina, and he was hoping to return to Chile to pick up some personal effects and spend some time with his mistress.

"I *need* this man," said his mistress, easily shedding a flurry of tears onto my desk. "You don't know what it's like."

I handed her a tissue and asked her some basic questions. I didn't know anyone in Argentina, so I asked the mistress to have Señor Reyes take a bus to Mendoza—an Argentinian city just across the mountains from Santiago—and I would meet him there.

On the appointed day, I took a bus across the Andean pass (a six-hour drive in the pre-Pinochet era, which took almost eight hours due to lengthy interrogations at the border crossing). I met Señor Reyes at a bar that evening. I had no trouble recognizing his bulbous nose and chin-length hair. We ordered a drink and a large bowl of mussels to share.

"Remind me, which mistress was it that sent you?" he asked, without a trace of arrogance.

"How many are there?"

Señor Reyes wagged a finger at the barman, who came over to refresh our glasses. The writer reached for another mussel, and I understood that he would not be answering my question.

I had spent the last few days trying to obtain a false Chilean passport for Señor Reyes but had not had any luck.

"We'll need to go to Buenos Aires," I said, "to get you an Argentinian passport."

"I'm not Argentinian," Señor Reyes protested.

"I'm aware."

We took a bus to Buenos Aires, where we wandered around the seedier parts of town asking questions that led us from one establishment to another. Eventually, we found a man—he told us his name was Ratón—who promised that, for a considerable fee, he could get us a passport in two days' time.

Señor Reyes and I took a room at a cheap inn and spent the better part of the next two days drinking and walking around Buenos Aires. I found myself helplessly drawn to him—he possessed the charisma and *bonhomie* often lacking in the few writers I had met. I was not the only one to be charmed by him; each of the two nights we spent in Buenos Aires I slept alone in our shared room, while he returned in the mornings with unbounded energy and the desire to take a long, hot shower.

When I had given up hope on ever hearing from him again, Ratón called and told us where to pick up the passport. We followed his directions and ended up at what appeared to be a brothel.

"Gentlemen, gentlemen," said an elderly woman, handing us each a glass of wine. It was not yet noon, and I couldn't even look at the wine. Señor Reyes took a sip of the wine and kissed the elderly woman's hand.

"Oh, dear," she said. "Now, isn't that lovely!"

She led us into a larger room, furnished with a small card table and several sprawling sofas. The room was filled with women of all types—large and small, tall and short, dark-skinned and light, brunette and not. The only commonality they shared was a tendency to be wearing only the most minimal clothing. Three of the women were seated around the table, thoroughly engaged in whatever card game they were playing.

"You deal with the passport," Señor Reyes whispered, "I'm going to go play cards."

The elderly woman took my arm and led me over to a young woman who was idly flipping through a magazine on the couch.

"This one seems like she would be to your liking, wouldn't you say?"

"I'm sorry," I said, "I haven't been clear. We're here because Ratón sent us to pick something up."

"Ratón!" exclaimed the elderly woman. She pulled me away from the young woman and hurried me over to a small adjoining room.

"What is it that you're here for?" she said briskly, taking a seat behind a large desk.

I explained that we were picking up a passport for my companion. The woman pushed her chair back and began rifling through one of the lower desk drawers. She muttered to herself as she pulled out a couple of passports and studied their pictures. She showed one to me and asked what I thought.

"This looks nothing like him," I said. "Look at the nose."

She showed me another one. I took a look at it and sighed.

"You need to be creative," she said. "There are things you can do to change his appearance."

She went back to looking through the drawer. After a minute or so, she gave a satisfied grunt and slid a passport across the desk. I opened it and nodded my reluctant assent.

"Then it's settled!" said the woman.

We haggled a bit over the price (though it would be Señor Reyes' mistress who paid the bill), and, when we were both somewhat satisfied, we left her office. Señor Reyes was sitting at the card table in a state of complete nudity. The other girls were either naked themselves or nearly so.

"I think I'm winning," Señor Reyes said, winking at me.

"Look at *you!*" said the elderly woman, her eyes shamelessly roving.

"I'm afraid, ladies, that it's time for me to go," Señor Reyes said, stooping to pick up his clothes. I turned away—too late, unfortunately—and headed for the door.

That evening, we took a bus back to Mendoza, where we spent much of the next day trying to alter Señor Reyes' appearance to make him resemble the passport photo. At the barbershop, Señor Reyes complained that losing his long hair could have disastrous Samson-like consequences. We found a cheap pair of reading glasses at a pharmacy and a false mustache at a magic shop.

The next morning, we boarded a bus to Santiago. Crossing the Andes in the wintertime is something everyone should experience at least once. The bus wound its way through the snow-capped *Cordillera*, allowing us unfettered views of forests and rivers.

At the border, the officer did not give us a second glance (or a first glance, for that matter—it seemed that any of the passports the elderly woman showed me would have sufficed), and, before we knew it, the bus was pulling into Santiago's busy downtown station.

"You're on your own now," I said, "for the next week."

Señor Reyes rubbed his hands together happily, and I gave him the name of the mistress who had hired me. I hoped that he would remember to go see her at least once.

The week passed somewhat uneventfully (for me—I'm sure Señor Reyes had his hands full), though I did receive a call early one morning from his mistress, who breathlessly thanked me over and over again for returning her lover to her. On the appointed day, I met Señor Reyes at his hotel. I sat down on his bed and waited while he shaved and glued on the false mustache. He would be flying to Buenos Aires, I explained, as the Andean border crossing had been temporarily closed due to a snowstorm.

I used the telephone to call down to reception and asked them to put me through to the airport. Once connected, I spoke to an agent for LanChile airlines and explained that I was the handler for Mr. Such-and-such, the current star of Argentina's most popular soap opera, and that he would be flying to Buenos Aires that afternoon. He would be somewhat disguised, I said, but they should still be prepared for some disruptions due to love-struck fans.

Señor Reyes and I took a taxi to the airport. I asked the taxi driver to turn on the radio and then quietly briefed Señor Reyes on the upcoming Manipulation. When we arrived, we got in line at the LanChile counter. We were nearly at the front of the line when a young woman came up and breathlessly asked if he was Mr. Such-and-such, and she was his biggest fan, and could she take a picture with him. She was quite convincing—one of my most promising students—though she did at one point fan herself with one hand, which I thought was a bit much. I could see the LanChile agents exchanging nods with another, and I knew they had been warned by whomever I had spoken to on the phone.

When Señor Reyes and I finally reached the desk, he handed over his passport and winked over the top of his glasses at the agent. She ran the passport through the computer and frowned. Then she tried it again and was again not happy with the results. I knew better than to trust people like Ratón and the madam, and so I reached over to put my briefcase on the ground. At that signal, a pair of women ran over and began squealing over Mr. Such-and-such. They made quite a commotion, and soon a couple of other women (and a man, simply because he was my least favorite student and I thought it important for him to do things that might make him uncomfortable) stampeded over and began clutching and shrieking at Señor Reyes. If I pulled my hat off my head, one of them would faint.

I asked the LanChile agent for some leeway, and Señor Reyes asked her if she might want to have dinner with him next time he was in Santiago, and the others were shrieking—the agent did not know how to deal with having everyone talking at her, so she hastily waved us through. Señor Reyes was escorted directly to his gate by an agent while I held back his adoring fans with promises of signed photographs.

Several years later, I received in the mail a copy of Señor Reyes' latest book. He had named a character in it "Javier Gonzalez"—not a particularly lovable character, but it was still a nice gesture. His inscription on the front page read: "To Javier, who gave me a week in my homeland when I needed it most. With lots of love, Mr. Such-and-such."

# FORTY-THREE

I spent the rest of the afternoon in the Library's Staff Only room. I worked on a cassette tape labeled "ARE YOU LISTENING TO ME?" and then turned to editing and transcribing the testimonies given by the tortured political prisoners.

Dinner was an uneventful affair, and I went to bed as soon as I could. I awoke a few hours later, at what must have been close to midnight. The moon was only half full but bright, and I tread quickly down the silent roads of the Colony. When I arrived at the goat barn, I fed the goats a pile of apples to calm their bleating. I called out Tibor's name as loud as I dared until he returned a groggy whisper.

"Is there a guard around?" I asked.

"They patrol every hour or so at night."

I looked around. "Where do they approach from?"

"The main road," Tibor said. "With a flashlight, always. You keep your eyes out, you can't miss them."

"I brought you a chicken sandwich," I said. "It's coming over the fence now." I lobbed the paper bag over to where Tibor was sitting. It landed on a pile of hay.

"When are we leaving?" Tibor said. "I'm ready to kill that guard who's here in the daytime."

"Sunday," I said. "I'm working on the plan, but I need your help. Look in the bag."

Tibor opened the bag. He pulled out a chicken sandwich, wrapped in two layers of thick wax paper. There was another object in the bag, wrapped in a sock.

"It's a tape recorder," I said. "I need a recording of you talking. I'll explain later. You can talk about whatever you want—just know that Uncle Peter is going to be listening to it."

"I've got lots of things to say to—"

"Start saying them, then," I interrupted. "I don't know how much time we have until the guards come around."

I found a place where I could sit with my back against a willow tree and keep an eye out on the road. Ten minutes or so must have gone by, and all I could hear was the low murmur of Tibor's voice coming from the barn. I must have nodded off, because the next thing I knew, there was the sound of laughter and the bouncing beams of a pair of flashlights rapidly approaching. I hissed a word of warning to Tibor. He switched off the tape recorder and buried it under a pile of hay.

I climbed up the willow as high as I could, my heart beating wildly and my breath coming in short gasps. It was not the ideal tree for hiding—I soon discovered—for lack of foliage, but it had to make do. I tried to take slow, deep breaths and to be as still as possible.

The guards shone their flashlights around the barn.

"What did it sound like?" said one of them, who I recognized to be Leonardo.

"Somebody talking—I couldn't hear what they were saying," said the other. "Here, let's look around."

At this, Tibor snored loudly and rolled around. He was trying to distract them. I had nowhere to go—I was treed.

The guards split up and circled the barn, playing their flashlights everywhere. They expanded outwards, tracing concentric circles. I tried to make myself as small as possible. There was an approaching noise and then stillness. I opened my eyes. It was Leonardo. I gave him an apologetic look and brought a finger up to my lips. He paused and then kept walking.

I closed my eyes and held my breath as they continued to search. I heard footsteps and then a satisfied grunt. I opened my eyes—there was a beam of light on my feet. It moved up my legs and up to my face. It was the guard who had shown me to my room and scattered my clothes. He grinned.

"Well, well, well," he said.

# FORTY-FOUR

The guard marched me over to the same room I was taken to when I first arrived at the colony. He pushed me into the room and warned me that there would be someone posted outside. I paced around for a few minutes, at first berating myself for having fallen asleep, and then working to come up with a strategy for facing Uncle Peter. I knew that being defensive would make things worse—I would have to go on the offensive from the very beginning. When I was overcome by the need to sleep, I stretched out flat on my back on the concrete floor. I took my handkerchief out of my pocket and put it beneath my head.

When I awoke, the room was bathed in early morning sunlight. I groaned and rolled over onto my side. That's when I noticed that Uncle Peter was standing at the window, looking out. It was a pose that looked affected—and probably was. He didn't say anything for several long moments, and I rolled myself into a sitting position.

"What the hell is going on?" he said, finally.

"I can—"

"You were visiting the Jew at midnight," he said, coldly. This was not the preaching Uncle Peter or the jovial,

219

punishing Uncle Peter—this was the laconic, ex-Nazi Uncle Peter.

"You're lucky we're here," Uncle Peter continued, "and not in the interrogation room."

I shuddered at the thought. I rubbed my arms briskly and tried to look alert—I had to take charge of this situation.

"I'm an actor," I said, "which means that I lie to people for a living."

Uncle Peter turned around.

"What it also means," I continued, "is that I can spot a liar a mile away. And the Jew is lying to us when he says that nobody helped him kill Dr. Koehler."

"We're not here to talk about the Jew!"

"You're right," I said, which is what I always say when trying to win someone over. "We're not. But do you know what I did last night? I brought him a chicken sandwich. And earlier that day? An apple. I'm trying to earn his confidence by bringing him food and talking to him, and, once he trusts me, then I can just peel back the layers of lies, and we'll get to the truth."

"This is not some sort of amateur operation, where everyone does what they want!" he said.

"I should have asked you," I said. "It was wrong to do this without telling you—but I thought you wanted to figure out who helped him kill Dr. Koehler, and I wanted to help."

"You think it's easy, what I do? You think some big shot from Santiago can walk into this place and start extracting information from anyone?"

I shook my head. "I wouldn't presume—I've been learning a lot from you in my short time here, is all. You've shown me things."

"I've seen lots of people," Uncle Peter said. "A few have what it takes, but most don't. You don't have what it takes."

"If you just gave me a chance—"

"I don't want to have you brought to my attention again."

I lowered my gaze. "Please accept my apologies."

"You are very quickly wearing out your welcome here."

# FORTY-FIVE

I made my way over to the library after breakfast. Ernesto was sweeping the floor. We were standing by the window when Greta walked by—her posture perfect, her stride determined.

"What is it with her?" I said.

Ernesto tipped the contents of his dustbin into a garbage can. "She and Angela were as close as any two people can be. She didn't used to be like this—she was an entirely different person before Angela passed away."

"She was here from the very beginning?"

"From even before that. She was a young woman living on a farm when Peter came by—before he was Uncle Peter. He had just begun his travels in the German countryside, and Greta's farm was one of the first places he stayed. He stayed in their barn for two weeks, borrowing one of their horses every day to ride into town and try to convert the people there. Greta fell in love with him and followed him everywhere he went, from barn to barn, town to town, onto a train that traversed Europe and a boat that wound its way across the Atlantic Ocean."

"It was not reciprocal," I said.

Ernesto chuckled. "How could it be?"

We went outside to gather up the chickens and started down the road. We veered off onto a trail that skirted along the edge of the forest. We circled around and ended up near the goat barn.

"Let's go see Tibor," I suggested.

Ernesto shook his head. "We can't get any closer," he said. "For some reason, these chickens love the smell of a goat barn, and they'll fly right over the electrified fence. I've never seen anything like it. It takes quite a bit of effort to get them out."

Something clicked into place. "How *do* you get them out?"

"Well," Ernesto said, "it happened only the one time. We had to turn off the electrified fence and get right in there."

One of my chickens stopped to peck at a plant. I let her work on it for a few moments. Then I jiggled the worm in front of her, and she immediately forgot about the plant and continued walking.

"How are you feeling about going home?" Ernesto said, breaking the silence.

His question took me by surprise. I had not given much thought to going home. All I had been focusing on was the escape itself and the logistics involved with the Manipulation. It took me some time before I was able to formulate an answer.

"There are things I love about the Colony," I said. "Most of them are things I never knew I would love. There's the physical labour, for one—working in the fields, preparing breakfast. There's a physical sense in which it makes me feel good, a bodily sense, but there's also the mental benefits of it. The feeling that I'm doing something that is concrete and useful, not abstract and often worthless, like teaching a man to feign embarrassment or to project his voice."

Ernesto nodded. We were at a fork in the road, and he pointed for us to go right—he didn't want to interrupt me.

"I like being told what to eat and when to eat it—what to prepare for breakfast and how to do it."

"You don't mind decisions being made for you," Ernesto said.

"It's more than that—I *want* these decisions made for me. There are too many micro-decisions that we make each day, and I'd just as rather not make most of them. I used to think that the more choices we have in our lives, the better—but now I think it might be the other way around."

A crowd of boys came marching down the trail, their instructor excitedly pointing out the names of plants. The children ignored him for the most part, but two of the boys were absorbing every word, walking wide-eyed and asking questions. When they were past us, Ernesto and I didn't speak again for several minutes.

"This place could be great," I said, "if it weren't run by a madman."

Ernesto nodded, not taking his eyes off his chickens.

"He's a brilliant manipulator," I said. "He's constantly uniting the colonists against a common enemy—the nuns at times, Tibor the Jew, their own traitorous colonists who have sinned too often, the cesspool that is Santiago, and essentially anywhere outside the Colony. Now he's not all wrong on that last one—Santiago *can* be a bit of a cesspool, and the rest of the country is run at the whim of another madman."

Uncle Peter's rule over the Colony and General Pinochet's rule over Chile were not so different. They were each running Manipulations of their own, at a far greater scale than I had ever thought possible.

I spent a long time in the fields that afternoon—the sun had taken a short leave of absence, and it was a bit chilly. I was happy to be outside, and, after my conversation with Ernesto that morning, I couldn't help thinking about the fact that I had only a couple of days left here. I wasn't sure what life would be like if I managed to escape from the Colony—only that it would somehow be different at a very basic level. I thought back to my daydream from a few days ago—the one with Elena and working in our garden while Claudio plays his clarinet for us—and it occurred to me that the only way to have that vision realized would be to stop limiting my relationships with those who cared for me. I was only limiting my own life by keeping the ties that bound me to others long and slack.

After dinner, the colonists trickled out of the dining hall while the children who would be in the play stayed behind. Their excitement was palpable, but there was an underlying sense of anxiety about the performance. For most of these children, this would be their first time ever performing on stage, and the fact remained that we had not yet rehearsed the play in its entirety.

"Let me start out by saying," I said, "that this play is not about memorizing lines and knowing exactly what part of the stage to come in from. What we're after is to have some fun and to entertain our fellow colonists."

This alone seemed to relieve some of the tension that had fallen over the room.

"I need you to remember that this play is a story that we're telling, and each chapter of the story will be loosely told. Now let's see how well you can remember—what's the first act?"

"Uncle Peter is born!" someone called out.

"Good, excellent. And what needs to happen during that act?"

One of the girls raised her hand—she was taller than any of the boys and had long black hair pulled into twin braids. It was Maca—who had helped me with my storytelling. "His mama can't get to the hospital in time so she makes the baby in a farm."

"That's right," I said. "And who plays the farmer?"

One of the boys raised his hand.

"The mother?"

A girl raised her hand.

"The doctor?"

Another girl.

"The barn animals?"

The rest of the kids raised their hands.

"Perfect," I said. "Second act?"

"Uncle Peter grows up!"

"And what happens in that act?"

In this way, we worked through the play, filling in any roles that were not filled and making sure that the children had a basic understanding of what the action was for each act.

"And now," I said, "time for the most important question."

All of the children quieted down.

"Who wants to be the director?"

The children looked at each other and then at me. Nobody said anything. I studiously avoided looking at Maca. Finally, she raised her hand. "*You're* the director!" she said, exasperated.

"Oh no," I said. "I'm the producer, playwright, and choreographer—I don't think I could take on the director role as well."

"Fine," Maca said, sighing. She could not have been more than 11 years old. "I'll do it."

# FORTY-SIX

I woke up on Saturday morning with a sense of immediacy and a feeling of unbridled energy. It might have been the same burst of energy that a runner stores until the very end of a race. I took a quick shower and put on my freshly laundered clothes. On Friday evenings, the residents of my dormitory would leave their clothes just outside our doors, and, on Saturday mornings, they were replaced with a clean set. The shirt I pulled on was a little stiff—it needed to be worked in—but I was otherwise feeling loose and relaxed and ready for my last full day in the Colony.

I arrived at the kitchen early, and Anita was cracking several trays of eggs into a gigantic bowl. She asked me to take over for her, and I was happy to do so.

"What are we making today?" I asked.

"We've got breakfast beans this morning," she said, not caring to elaborate more on what that might be, "and what you're working on there is going to be kuchen."

Anita showed me a book on German cooking—it had a blackened cover and stained pages.

"I'm putting you in charge of the apple kuchen," Anita said. She opened the book and showed me the recipe (which she, in pencil, had translated from the German, and adapted to fit the large scale of the Colony).

I put the heavy cookbook down on the table and summoned the reserves of energy that I had awoken with that morning.

Anita said, "The ovens are preheating already."

I must have had a look on my face, because she grabbed the scruff of my neck and pulled on it gently.

"You're ready for this," she said.

I snagged a passing colonist and asked her to measure out the many cups of flour and to then add the baking powder and salt to that mixture. A man came up and asked me if he could help, and I asked him to start chopping apples.

I found a stack of oversized baking pans and oiled them. Then I stopped and looked around the kitchen. It was not so different than directing a play, this business of making food on a large scale. As long as everyone played their role, they would be making a lot of people happy.

Anita came by to check on things and to congratulate me on a job well done.

"So long as you don't burn it," she said, smiling.

I planted myself in front of the oven for the entire cooking time, anxious to not overcook the kuchen.

"Apple kuchen," Ernesto said–later, when we were leaving the dining hall, "was Angela's favorite breakfast."

The kuchen had been a hit—people had come by for seconds and thirds, and, next thing I knew, it was all gone.

"It's the other reason I can't leave the Colony," Ernesto said. "Angela is here. She's in that sign, in the woods where we would go for walks, and in the river we swam in—she's everywhere. If I leave, all those memories will trickle away. And there's her grave, too, of course, and mine."

I went to visit Tibor. It was risky but necessary. I found him sitting morosely on the floor, tearing at bits of straw and abjectly petting one of the goats who was curled up next to him.

I waited at a distance until a group of onlookers left, and then I asked him how he was doing.

"I'm too old for all this," he groaned, stretching his neck.

I nodded sympathetically.

"It wasn't bad at first—I was so happy to be alive. Now I'm getting a bit fed up with suckling and being called names and having apples thrown at me."

"I can't stay long," I said. "I got in trouble for visiting you. But tomorrow is going to be a big day."

Tibor's face brightened.

"I'm going to need your help," I said. "Have you got anything to swing at a man with?"

Tibor nodded seriously.

"Great," I said. "Keep it handy." I told him when I'd be coming by and what to do.

Tibor brought a hand up to scratch at his head, and the goat that he was petting began bleating and nudging him with her nose. He resumed his duties, and she happily tried to lick her eye with a surprisingly long tongue.

I pulled a paper bag out from my pocket and tossed it over the fence. Tibor opened it up and pulled out a large slice of kuchen.

"From breakfast," I said.

Tibor took a bite and made a face. "It's a bit dry," he said.

"I made it."

"It would be heavenly with a tall glass of goat milk," Tibor said, apologetically.

"The tape recorder—" I said, "I need it back."

He fished it out from some hidden nook and lobbed it over the fence.

A group of children was approaching, and I made a hasty departure.

# FORTY-SEVEN

"Cut! Stop!"

Greta obeyed, reluctantly silencing her musicians with the flick of a wrist. Then she turned slowly with a scowl on her face.

"That was *much* too fast," Maca said. "Let's try it again, but this time I want the music to be slower."

Greta glowered at me, and I shrugged.

"Action!" Maca yelled. A young boy dressed in overalls began skipping across the stage. He carried a cardboard guitar in hand, and was pretending to strum it. Greta cued the band, and they began to play a high-spirited German folk tune.

"It's too loud," Maca said, jotting down something in the notepad I had given her. We were sitting together on a pew, while the rest of the cast and the musicians tried to run through the play without getting interrupted.

On the stage, the boy who was playing a young Uncle Peter stopped skipping. He approached a group of farmers and animals that were sitting in a circle on bales of hay. Greta brought her hand down, and the band lowered its volume down to a whisper.

"Hi, folks!" he said.

"Hi," said the farmers, as well as some of the animals.

"I'm Uncle Peter, and I'm here to teach you about God and those things."

"Oh, good!"

In this way, the young Uncle Peter managed to convince the farmer and his animals that they were living a life of sin and that, by accepting God and Uncle Peter, they would be blessed.

"Cut!" yelled Maca, shooting out of her seat and towards the stage. She began lecturing the young Uncle Peter on how to show more enthusiasm and excitement. I walked over to the right of the stage, where Claudio was holding up one of the scenery backdrops. I adjusted something that did not need adjusting. I had decided not to tell him anything about the escape tomorrow—it would only make him anxious, and I didn't want him to let anything slip to any of the other children.

"When are we leaving?" Claudio said, when he saw it was me.

"Any day now," I said. "You've got to be ready at any moment."

"My mom," he said. "She . . . she . . . I don't want to be a Sprinter." His voice cracked. I looked down at his hands. He had been picking at his knuckles—they were swollen and raw.

"We're so close," I said. "I need you to hang in there. Your mom needs you to hang in there—okay?"

"My dad didn't want me to come here," he said

This was the first I had heard of any of this—Elena had not said much about Claudio's father.

Claudio's eyes were darting around the room. "The other boys say that, on the first night, Uncle Peter takes you into the bath with him. You have to wash him. He . . ."

Claudio couldn't get the rest of the sentence out. His breathing was erratic.

"Look at me," I said, squatting next to him.

He did.

"I'll get you out of her before you ever become a Sprinter. I give you my word—now breathe slowly and deeply."

I sent him to the bathroom to calm down and wash his face. Then I went around to the front of the stage. Maca was demonstrating to the young Uncle Peter how to skip like he meant it. I persuaded her to let them run through the scene without any further interruptions, and we sat back down to watch the young Uncle Peter comically win over a group of farmers and unidentifiable animals. The act ended with him skipping away and all of them skipping in a line after him.

We proceeded through the play, making sure that people more or less knew what they were doing and that Greta and the band knew when to play which bits of music. It was not altogether a bad performance, especially given the minimal amount of time that we had to work on it.

Maca sighed loudly and wrote something down in her notebook. "Let's try this again—from the beginning!" she yelled.

# FORTY-EIGHT

I tossed and turned all night, falling in and out of a shallow sleep—the kind of sleep that does not really feel like sleep at all. In the end, I got out of bed an hour earlier than necessary and took a long, hot shower. I sat on the edge of my bed and tried to relax my entire body, muscle by muscle. When I was done, I went over to my bag, in the corner of the room—where it had remained since my arrival. I pulled out a few necessary items (my ID card, money, some photographs) and put them in my pockets. I looked around the room; if all went as planned, I would not be setting foot in here again.

Anita greeted me as soon as I entered the kitchen. "I need your help," she said. She handed me a cookbook and opened it to a recipe for carrot muffins. I nodded and went to find some willing helpers to wash and grate several pounds of carrots. In this way, the next hour flew by: the carrots had to be soaked in lemon juice; butter had to be melted; walnuts had to be chopped; raisins had to be added to the batter—

"Hold on!" Anita came rushing over.

"What is it?" I said, looked around.

"The raisins," she said. "There are raisins in the recipe."

"Yes—"

"Have you added them?"

I pointed at the oversized mixing bowl in front of me. The raisins had just been added but had not been stirred in yet. Anita wiped her brow and sagged against the counter.

"He hates raisins."

"Who?"

"We have to pick them all out."

Most of the raisins were easy to remove, but some had begun to sink into the soft, gooey batter. I rolled up my sleeves, and Anita did the same. We worked side by side, arms deep into the mixing bowl, squeezing batter-coated chunks between our fingers to figure out if they were walnut bits or raisins.

"He hates raisins?" I asked.

"All dried fruit," Anita said.

"Then why do we even have raisins here?"

"When he's gone," Anita said, "sometimes I like to add them to dessert. Everyone else loves them."

The carrot muffins went into the oven at the last possible moment, and, when they emerged, they were shuttled straight to the serving table. When most people had sat down to eat their breakfast, I went to ask Uncle Peter if I could make an announcement.

"It's about the play," I said.

"This carrot muffin," he said. "It smells like raisins."

"Smells like raisins?"

"It does," he said. "Here."

I dutifully smelled it. "Have you found a raisin?"

"Not so far."

"Well, then, I don't know how it could smell like raisins."

"Make your announcement already," Uncle Peter said.

I got up and clapped my hands to get everyone's attention. "THIS AFTERNOON, DIRECTLY AFTER LUNCH, WE WILL ALL GO TOGETHER TO THE CHURCH," I called out, cupping my hands around my mouth, "FOR THE BIG PERFORMANCE OF THE FIRST PLAY EVER TO BE HELD AT THE COLONY. IT IS THE STORY OF UNCLE PETER'S LIFE AND OF THE COLONY!"

Uncle Peter raised an arm up into the air like a bullfighter, and everyone cheered. He stood up, and the cheering stopped. "Attendance is mandatory," he added, and then sat back down.

Once back in the kitchen, I ate three of the carrot muffins and decided to forfeit my daily bowl of oatmeal. I had a lot to do, and being a bit hungry would help me do it. The post-breakfast crew began cleaning up, and I went to find Anita. She was in the walk-in cooler, picking tomatoes out of a box and placing them carefully in the fold of her apron.

"Would you grab as many of those as you can carry?" she asked. I obliged, balancing several tomatoes in the crook of one arm. We walked back out to the sink, and Anita began washing them, one by one.

"I just wanted to thank you for letting me make those things the last couple of days," I said. "The kuchen and the carrot muffins."

Anita looked up, surprised. "I'm the one who should be thanking you."

Neither of us said anything for a moment.

"I don't understand how you do this," I said. I couldn't look at her—it was not a fair thing to say to someone.

"It's not a choice," Anita said. "If it was a choice, it would be hard. But it's surprisingly easy to grow accustomed to situations that are outside of your control."

"Someday, you're going to get your little restaurant," I said, putting an arm around her and squeezing her shoulder.

"Run along now," she said. "It's a beautiful day out there."

She was right—the sun was beaming down on the Colony, and there wasn't a cloud in the sky. Ernesto was sitting on the front porch of the library, just like he had been on my very first day. He was impatiently waiting for me to arrive so that we could take the chickens out for a walk.

"Just a very short walk for now," I said. "We'll need them to have lots of energy later on."

# FORTY-NINE

I spent the rest of the morning putting the finishing touches on the escape plan and gathering the tools I would need. When the lunch bell rang, I followed Ernesto out of the library and into the dining hall. We lined up to fill our plates with shepherd's pie, a grated beet salad, and a small cup of fruit salad.

A woman confessed to sneaking food into her room for a midnight snack, and a man confessed to having tricked a fellow colonist into doing his bathroom chore for him. I finished eating and headed over to the Church. The set was almost completely up, and most of the children were in the costumes they would be wearing for the first act. There were jitters to ease and self-confidences to build, and I walked among the children and did my best.

"Listen up, folks," I said, waving everyone over. "I want to remind you of a couple of things. Number one—we are here to have fun. The audience is going to have a good time, they're going to laugh and clap, and they're going to love every minute of it. Number two—I'm not your director. Maca, here, is your director. She knows what's going on, so take your cues from her."

The band began noisily tuning their instruments, and the children dispersed, clustering in small groups to tug at each others' costumes and go over what they would be doing on stage. Maca came over and thanked me for reminding everyone about her very important role. The colonists had begun filing into the Church, and I went to ensure that they were all filling the seats up at the front first. When everyone was seated (with Uncle Peter prominently in the front row), I went up to the front of the stage.

"Welcome, my fellow colonists," I began. I looked out into the sea of white shirts and dark-print skirts, of bonnets and suspenders.

"I am delighted to bring you the very first play that has ever been performed at the Colony. It is the story of Uncle Peter and of how the Colony came to be. The actors have worked very hard, as have the wonderful volunteers who helped with the set and costumes, and Greta's hard-working orchestra. Let's give them our full attention. And now, without further ado, I urge you to sit back and enjoy the first and only performance of "How We All Ended Up Here.""

The audience applauded dutifully, and I went backstage. A girl walked too quickly across the stage, holding up a sign that read "Act One: The Birth." A boy came out riding a broomstick with a papier-mache horse head stuck on it.

"I'm Uncle Peter's father!" cried the boy. He had a yarn beard pasted on his face, and he looked terrified. Greta tapped her baton against her music stand, and the flutes section began playing a happy German folk tune. The other instruments joined in, and the boy on stage began to look more comfortable.

"Today's the day I'm going to become a father," said the boy, galloping across the stage. "My wife is going to have a baby. That baby is going to someday be Uncle Peter!"

A table and chairs were carried out onto one side of the stage, and a girl with a pillow stuffed under her dress came out.

"Oh, husband!" she cried out. "This baby is ready to come out. Come home, so you can take me to the doctor!"

The boy took his cue and galloped over to where the girl was doing a good job of feigning agony. "I'm home, wife," he said. "Now, hop on my horse, and I will take you to the doctor's house."

The girl struggled to her feet and mounted the wooden broomstick. The boy took off without giving her any warning, and she was left to run after him.

"Oh, husband!" she ad-libbed, "go slower, please. I'm pregnant, don't forget." She put her hands on the boy's shoulders to prevent him from hurrying away, and, soon, they were prancing happily around the stage, dropping her pillow only once (to the audience's delight).

A crowd of farmers and animals came onto the stage carrying a large bale of hay.

"This baby can't wait!" said the girl. "It's coming out now—look, there's a farm. Let's stop, so I can have my baby there."

The band began playing an ominous tune. The farmers and animals excitedly made a ring around the girl while she yelled and wailed for far too long—Maca was in the wings frantically signaling for her to give birth already. When the crowd pulled back, the pillow was gone and the girl held a doll in her arms. The trumpet section played a triumphant fanfare. The girl held the doll up to the audience and said, "I shall name him Uncle Peter!"

The audience cheered, and I saw Uncle Peter smile genuinely for the first time. The actors hurried offstage in the midst of the applause. A boy walked solemnly across the stage with a sign—"Act 2: A Traveling Young Man."

A boy skipped out onto the stage, strumming on a cardboard guitar. Greta cued the band into another bouncing folk tune. The boy stopped at center stage and addressed the audience. "I'm Uncle Peter," he said, "at the age of nineteen!" He continued skipping, and the same crowd of farmers and animals scurried onto stage left. The boy noticed them and skipped over.

"Well, hello there," he said cheerfully.

They responded with a dejected chorus of "Hi's" and "Hello's."

"You don't sound very happy," said the boy.

One of the farmers stepped forward. "We're not," he said. "It's hard to make a living these days, and we don't have any spiritual connection to our world."

"Oh, boy," said the boy. "Have I got good news for you!"

He began extolling the virtues of loving each other and a higher power; he told them about his vision: a self-sustaining community where people would be free to farm and live and love each other without the pressures and dangers of the outside world. The farmers and animals grew increasingly excited, and the band played louder and louder, until everyone began jumping around on stage in time to the music and—under Maca's furious gesturing—they finally skipped offstage together.

In Act Three, a series of chairs were lined up on the stage, and the children played passengers on a train that kept getting filled with more and more soon-to-be colonists. Some people in the audience hollered—presumably those who had been on that train. Then the set was transformed by bobbing layers of cardboard blue waves, and the children were on a boat crossing the Atlantic. I poked my head around the curtain to take another look at Uncle Peter. He seemed to be enjoying himself, tapping his foot along to the intermittent music and occasionally nodding in recognition or approval.

"Act Four: Finding Our Home" began with a young Uncle Peter buying up a piece of land from a businessman wearing an oversized suit. The crowd of followers—who, by this point in the play, were literally following him around on stage everywhere he went—began to cheer. They picked him up on their shoulders and marched him around the fenced area that represented the earliest incarnation of the Colony. The band played another triumphant tune, and the real Uncle Peter couldn't hold back from throwing his fist into the air. The audience gave him a standing ovation—the children, believing it was for them, took a long set of uncoordinated bows, looking remarkably like a huddle of penguins.

In the next act, Uncle Peter bought adjacent pieces of land from other farmers (and one particularly happy group of nuns). The children played the roles of current and past Colonists, much to the bemusement of the audience.

"I'm Anita the cook," said one little girl—the youngest of all the performers—in a white apron that dragged on the floor like a gown. "I make the goodest food in the world!"

"And I'm Ernesto the librarian," said a boy, "and my stories are funny!"

I put my arm around Maca's shoulders and told her that I would be stepping away for a moment. She looked up at me, her eyes fearful all of a sudden.

"Hey," I said, "who's the director here?"

"Me," she said in a small voice.

"Who's running the show?"

"I am."

"That's right," I said. "Now listen—you've done a great job so far. You've been running a tight ship, and I want you to keep doing that. Okay?"

Maca nodded. I began to walk away, but she hurried after me.

"You're coming back, right?"

"You can do this without me," I said. "You did it yesterday at the rehearsal. Everyone knows what they're doing—you just have to be there for them."

"Come back, though," Maca said.

# FIFTY

My knapsack was hiding backstage, under a platform—I picked it up and hefted it over my shoulders. I silently made my way around to the back of the Church, down the narrow set of stairs that led to the interrogation room. It was locked, as I expected it to be. I fished around in my knapsack until I found the tape recorder. I turned it on and heard Tibor's voice.

"Hi there, Uncle Peter. If you're listening to this, then our escape plan is already in motion. Soon enough I will be long gone from this godforsaken place, and you'll have to watch your back for every minute of every day, because you'll never know when I'm going to return for my revenge. In other news, I took great pleasure in killing your dear friend Dr. Koehler. Let me tell you about the look on his—"

I opened the slot at the bottom of the door and slipped the tape recorder through, pushing it off to one side. I made sure to leave the slot open, so you could just hear Tibor's voice leaking through. I went back upstairs—onstage, the children were growing pretend vegetables, building a hospital, etc.

Backstage, there were children running around excitedly, putting on costumes and whispering to each other. There was a panel in the very corner with all the light switches for the church. I flicked them all off with a swipe of my hand, then on again, then off, then on, and one more time, off and on. There was a murmur among the colonists, and those who were on stage paused for a moment. Then things returned to normal.

I peeked around the curtain. Uncle Peter was frowning—he looked confused. I waited a few moments and then repeated the procedure. Another murmur, and, once again, the children bravely continued with their performance. Uncle Peter put his hands on his knees and pushed himself up. He marched angrily down the aisle and to the staircase leading down to the basement. I followed him down the stairs and caught up with him just as he was approaching the interrogation room.

"Go back upstairs," he ordered.

"I did it!" I said.

He turned to me—slowly. "Did what?" he said, menacingly.

"Listen," I said. He paused. Tibor's voice floated up from the open slot at the base of the door. My heart was beating furiously, and I tried to convert that anxiety into anger.

"I cracked him," I said. "He's confessing—don't worry, I'm tape-recording it."

"Son of a bitch," Uncle Peter said. He pulled a key out of his pocket and twisted it in the lock.

He swung the door open and stepped inside. I pushed him into the room with both hands, as hard as I could. He stumbled onto the bed, and I yanked the door shut. The key was still in the lock, and I turned it until I heard a click. Then I pulled a hammer out of my knapsack and swung it, neatly snapping the key in two, leaving one end still in the lock. I slid the slot shut and pressed my ear against the door. There was a moment of quiet, and then there was the muffled sound of pounding on the door. The room was too heavily soundproofed for me to hear much. I leaned against the door. There were things I had to do—and fast—but there were also some things I had to say. The yelling stopped, and I squatted down by the slot and opened it.

"What the hell are you doing?" Uncle Peter said.

"Keep your hands off the children," I said.

"This is boring me—close the slot, and leave me in peace. The guards will come by soon. I'll come out, and then you and I can have a longer chat. Maybe in this very room."

"Oh, I'm not sure I'll want to return from Santiago just for that," I said.

"Santiago—ha! The guards have strict orders to never let anyone out of the Colony."

"Unless . . . ?" I said.

He grew silent.

"On another note," I said, "guess who helped Tibor kill your dear friend, Dr. Koehler?"

"You have no idea," Uncle Peter said. There was a lack of certainty in his voice that I had never heard before.

"It was me!" I said. "Now isn't that an interesting turn of events?"

"You're lying," he said, angrily.

"Tell you what," I said. "First thing you do when they let you out of there, is go to the kitchen, find yourself a fork, and then put out your other eye—because you just lost another goddamn race."

# FIFTY-ONE

I went back upstairs.

"Where were you?" Maca said, hitting my leg.

It was time for the final act. A girl walked across the stage—her sign read "Act Eight: Punishment." The band launched into a dissonant melody, and most of the children who were in the play walked onto the stage. They sat on the floor and pretended to talk amongst themselves, ignoring the audience. Maca entered stage right. She was dressed in black, and, in her hands, she held a small blackboard and a paddle. She prowled around the stage before smacking the paddle on the ground. The music stopped abruptly.

"I'm Aunt Petra," she said, "and sometimes I get a little bit grumpy."

Someone in the audience tittered. Everyone else craned their necks to look at the front row. They wanted to see how Uncle Peter would be taking it.

This was what lowering the worm stick looked like. I wanted the colonists to take a bite—they would finally see it wasn't a real worm at all but a rubber one.

"Now let me see here," Aunt Petra said, peering at the blackboard. There were names written on it. "Juanito!"

The children grew silent. One of them stood, timidly. He had his hands in his pocket, and his head was down.

"What have you done, Juanito?"

"I . . . I . . . nothing, Aunt Petra."

"Your name is on the list—you must have done something!"

I found Claudio backstage, watching through a gap in the curtain. "We're leaving the Colony," I said, "right this very minute."

He breathed in sharply and grabbed my hand. I led him out the back door of the Church and down the empty roads of the Colony.

Aunt Petra was going to spank Juanito with the paddle, and she was going to spank another child as well. The children were then going to realize that, if they refrained from putting each other's names on the blackboard, nobody would get punished. A little girl was going to walk up to Juanito and say, "You are not alone—we've got to work together." And Juanito would agree. As in Ernesto's monster story, the children were going to try to hug the evil out of Aunt Petra. When that failed, they were going to tie her up and throw her out of the Colony.

Ernesto was waiting a short distance outside of the goat barn, jostling around a worm stick to keep the attention of the small group of chickens that clustered around him.

"Time for your walk," Ernesto said, handing me a worm stick.

I led the chickens up to the goat barn—Claudio and Ernesto stayed behind. As I approached the barn, the chickens began clucking loudly and flapping their wings.

A guard came out from his post to see what was going on. It was the same guard who had made Tibor drink milk straight from the goat's teat.

"Nice day," I said to him.

"Why aren't you at the play?" he demanded.

"I was at the play," I said, "with Ernesto. One of us had to walk the chickens. I've seen the play at rehearsals a dozen times, and he hasn't seen it yet. Play or no play, these chickens got to have their walks."

I got closer to the goats, and the chickens began ignoring the worm sticks. Suddenly, one of them broke into a run, and the others quickly followed suit. The guard waved his arms and tried to get in their way, but the smell of the goat barn was much too alluring. One by one, the chickens flapped their wings and sailed over the electrified fence and into the barn. The goats began bleating uncomfortably at their unwanted guests, and the guard looked around helplessly. Tibor was lying on a pile of hay in the corner of the barn, pretending to sleep.

"Last time this happened, the goats all panicked and broke out of the barn," I said.

"God damn it!"

"You turn that fence off, and I'll get in there and corral up the ladies," I said. "I'll have them out of your hair in no time."

"You've got five minutes," said the guard, hefting his gun. "Then I'll start shooting them." He returned to his post and yelled that the fence was off. I climbed over the fence and floundered around in there for a few moments until the guard swore at me and came into the barn himself. I picked up one of the chickens, turning my body so I was facing Tibor. I pinned the chicken's wings down the way Ernesto had shown me. I asked the guard to come over, and I made a move to hand him the struggling chicken. He slung his gun over his shoulder and held his hands out.

Over the guard's shoulder, I saw Tibor stand up and dig out a broken two-by-four from his pile of hay. "Be gentle with her," I said. Just as the guard was about to close his hands over the chicken, I released her wings and she flapped them frantically in the guard's face. Tibor stepped forward and swung mightily at the guard's head. The impact knocked the guard off his feet. A trickle of dark, viscous blood crept down his face, and he looked like he was out cold. I took a length of rope out from my bag and passed it to Tibor, who knelt beside the guard and tied his hands and legs.

"Stuff this in his mouth," I said, handing Tibor a sock. He went over to one of the goats and rubbed the sock on its underside.

"There," he said, rolling the sock up and cramming it into the guard's mouth.

I produced a small container of chicken feed from my knapsack and poured some out onto the ground. The chickens waddled over and huddled together, happily pecking away at the food. When they were finished, I shook the container at them, and they followed me eagerly as I backed out of the barn and down the road. Tibor dragged the guard over to one of the birthing stalls and re-electrified the fence.

Ernesto and Claudio emerged from behind a tree. I pulled another length of rope from my bag and told Tibor to turn around.

"In case we come across a guard," I said, tying his hands.

We walked as quickly as we could back to the library and locked the chickens back in their coop. Then we went around to the back of Uncle Peter's office. The window out back was high off the ground. I handed Claudio the hammer and managed to get him sitting on my shoulders. We teetered over to the wall, and Claudio used it to steady himself while he shakily stood up.

"Now break that window," I said.

He tapped it gently—nothing happened.

"Come on, boy!" Tibor said.

Claudio cocked his arm back and smashed the hammer through the window, sending a shower of glass into the room.

"Knock in the rest of the glass," I said.

He did as he was told, and, after some urging, he hauled himself up and through the window frame. We went around to the front of the office, and Claudio was there, holding the door open. Uncle Peter's desk was neat and uncluttered. I shrugged my knapsack off my shoulders and handed it over to Ernesto. He rummaged around inside it until he found the tape player and a set of well-labeled tapes. He put these down on the desk and moved the phone to the center of the desk.

"Come here, old man," I said, pulling Ernesto towards me.

"You would have made a fine librarian," he said, his voice muffled into my chest.

"I'm going to miss you," I said. My throat caught—I was reminded of my father dying in the hospital and the way I looked at him carefully every night, thinking that I was seeing him for the last time. "Now have a seat, and wait for that phone to ring. Shouldn't be too long."

Ernesto sat down at Uncle Peter's desk and put his feet up. I herded Tibor and Claudio out the door and into the road.

# FIFTY-TWO

A nervous energy overtook me as soon as we stepped outside. I felt it inside me—that familiar cannonball in the stomach. Tibor seemed like he was doing okay—the man had survived a concentration camp and killed a man, and I did not worry about him much. Claudio was a different story. We walked quickly and silently, until we could just see the gate that was the only way in and out of the Colony. Claudio took my hand—I shook it loose and stopped walking. I squatted down in front of him and looked at him firmly.

"Now, listen," I said, "and listen carefully. Are you feeling afraid right now?"

Claudio nodded, avoiding my eyes.

"Is your heart going fast? Are you breathing harder?"

"I think so."

"Can you remember the last time you felt excited?"

Claudio shook his head.

I tried to remain calm. "Have you ever felt so excited that your heart started beating faster?"

"Yes," Claudio whispered.

"So excited that your breathing started getting harder?"

"Yes," he said, louder this time.

"I'm going to ask you one last question. The first time you rode a bike downhill—" I said, "how did that make you feel?"

Claudio closed his eyes. "Afraid," he said. "And excited."

"They're not as far from each other as we think they are. So here we are, moments away from freedom, on our way to go see your mother—now, doesn't that sound exciting?"

I put my hand on Tibor's shoulder and all three of us walked over to the guard post. I thought of how I had snuck Señor Reyes out of the country. "At my signal," I said, "when I blow my nose—all of us start talking at once," I said.

The others nodded.

"Where do you think you're going?" said the guard, stepping out.

"It's me, Javier," I said. "I've got the Jew with me. And Uncle Peter's newest soon-to-be Sprinter." I cuffed the top of Claudio's head. He whirled around and gave me a credible scowl.

The guard held up a hand to silence me. "What does any of this have to do with me?"

I took a step closer to the guard and motioned for him to lean forward.

"I don't want to say this too loud," I whispered, "for fear of startling the Jew—but Uncle Peter wants me to let the boy have his first kill."

The guard straightened up. "You mean the boy's going to—"

I shushed him and leaned forward again. "Have some decency," I said. "Even a Jew doesn't deserve to know that he's going to be killed by a boy."

The guard shook his head. "I can't let you through," he said. "You know the rules—nobody leaves the Colony."

I faked a yawn. "Tell you what," I said. "I just came from Uncle Peter's office. He's there right now—why don't you give him a call and see what he says?"

The guard reached into his office and pulled out a telephone. He held the base with one hand and the receiver with the other. He dialed the number for Uncle Peter's office.

"What is it?" Uncle Peter's voice crackled through the lines.

"Uncle Peter," said the guard, "I'm stationed at the front gate—there's a man trying to get the Jew and a boy out of here. He claims you've given them permission to walk out the gate."

"Javier is following my orders."

"With all due respect," said the guard, "you told us to never let anyone out of the Colony."

There was a short pause. I could imagine Ernesto changing from one tape to another.

"You will do as I say, or you will be severely punished!"

"But Uncle Peter, you've instructed us to keep anyone from leaving the Colony."

"Are you listening to me?"

"Yes, I—"

"I'm not talking just to hear the sound of my own voice!"

"I'm listening, Uncle Peter—it's just that you've told us one thing, and now you're telling me something else, and I just don't—"

"Stop it with your *stupid blabbering*! Are you going to make me repeat myself? You are nothing but a *clod of dirt*!"

There was poor Martha S., standing in the dining hall while Uncle Peter viciously attacked her. The phone connection went dead. The guard turned to look at us.

"You can go," he said. "But the boy stays."

"Uncle Peter said I get to kill the Jew," Claudio said, staring hard at the guard.

"What?" Tibor said.

"Call him again," I said. "I'm in no hurry."

The guard picked up the receiver and tapped it against his jaw.

I pulled my handkerchief out of my pocket and loudly blew my nose. Tibor and Claudio began talking to the guard—Tibor pleading for him not to let us out, Claudio asking to borrow his gun. I jumped in, telling the guard we'd be back in no time.

The guard yelled at us all to be quiet. He put the phone back in its cradle.

"It won't take long," I said helpfully.

The guard shook his head and opened the gate. I pushed Tibor roughly through the opening. Claudio followed behind. The gate slammed shut, and we walked in a line down the road.

"Don't anybody turn around," I said.

The road was dusty and dry, and we marched in silence for a few minutes. I took long, slow breaths. We walked single-file—like grandfather, father, and son, like elephants marching trunk to tail. I turned around to look at Claudio. He was somewhere between laughing and crying.

I put my hands on Tibor's shoulders and squeezed. A gust of wind blew past us, stirring up a dust cloud. A bud from a eucalyptus tree dropped onto the road from overhead. We rounded one corner and then another. There was a vehicle parked in the distance. I squinted—Julio and Rodolfo seemed to be playing cards on the hood of the car. They had not yet seen us.

"Only way to do this sort of thing," Tibor said. "You walk in, you walk out."

# FIFTY-THREE

We made it to Santiago in record time, stopping only once to buy a sack of sandwiches from a roadside stand. Claudio fell asleep, and we dropped Tibor off at a friend's house. He would need to vanish—I would help.

"You've got enough money to get you somewhere?" I asked. We were standing beside the car, outside of his friend's house. "Just until things blow over."

Tibor nodded. "I'll go to the bank tomorrow morning and then straight to the airport and on a plane to—"

I held up a hand to interrupt him. "It's better if I don't know where."

"You saved my life," Tibor said. "Thank you." He opened his arms and pulled me into a hug.

"We did it all of us together," I said, gesturing towards the car.

"Now, go get that boy home to his mother," Tibor said.

It was dinnertime when we arrived at Elena's apartment, and we were all ready to stretch our legs. We piled out of the car and into the lobby. Claudio waved at the doorman, and he let us in. Claudio's excitement was infectious, and I found myself full of an anticipation and eagerness that was probably not unrelated to Elena.

When Elena opened the door and found her son standing there, she let out a gasp. She swept Claudio up into her arms and kissed the top of his head.

"My baby," she said, her voice breaking.

When Elena finally let go, her face was streaked with tears. She looked up and came over to embrace me. I was waiting for an airport hug, but what I got was less than that—something like a ten-year high school-reunion hug.

"Thank you, thank you," she said. I could feel her wet cheeks through my shirt.

Elena pulled away and went over to hug Julio and Rodolfo. She ushered us into the apartment.

"We've interrupted your dinner," Julio said, gesturing at the table.

"Oh," Elena said. She blushed, and, just as I noticed that the table was set for two, there was a flush from the bathroom, and the door swung open. A man walked out, and Claudio hurried over to him. The man let out an exclamation—he picked up Claudio and hugged him tightly.

"That's Claudio's father," Elena said. She wouldn't look at me, and I felt very tired all of a sudden.

"Eduardo," the man said, coming over to vigorously shake all of our hands. "I can't thank you enough."

"We've both been so heartbroken," Elena said, looking at Julio. "Eduardo's been such a great help, and it seems that we're going to make another go at it. For Claudio's sake."

It would take hardly any work to break them up. I had a student who would play the perfect temptress, or one who could play a love child—there was any number of Manipulations I could run.

"Javier taught me how to act," Claudio said to his mother.

I looked down at the boy, and I realized that I wanted to be nothing like Uncle Peter, nothing like General Pinochet.

"How can I repay you for this?" Elena said.

"There's no need," I said.

"Please," Elena said. "You've given us our son back."

I looked at Julio and at Rodolfo. I looked at Eduardo, and he nodded eagerly, expectantly. But I had nothing more to say. I had reconstituted a family, brought them together—as an airport does. They were going to be happy, and I was going to be happy for them.

Julio cleared his throat. "It's been a long day," he said.

Claudio and I said our goodbyes, and he went off to the kitchen with his father. Elena walked us to the door. Julio pulled Rodolfo ahead, to wait for the elevator.

"Thank you for understanding," Elena said. She couldn't look at me, which was just as well, because I couldn't look at her, either.

"I'm standing here," Elena said, "trying to think of how I can cheer you up."

"I don't—"

She hugged me—tightly—the way people do at Departures. "This is all I can think of," she said.

I wanted to thank her, but I didn't trust my voice. Instead, I hugged her back and thought about her son, who had, indeed, turned out to be a fine actor.

In the car, Julio put his hand on my shoulder and squeezed. "I'm sorry," he said.

"I need to sleep," I said. "I'm fine."

I felt the same as I had when I got the call from the police about the car accident—like I wanted to snip away at every single tie that bound me to anyone. Julio, *snip*. Rodolfo, *snip*. My sister, *snip*.

"We can run a Manipulation and have them broken up in two weeks' time," Rodolfo said.

Julio took a hand off the steering wheel to slap Rodolfo's shoulder.

"What?" Rodolfo said.

"I'm taking you home, Javier" Julio said. "But Rodolfo and I are buying you lunch tomorrow."

I stared straight ahead.

"A *celebratory* lunch!" Julio said, emphatically.

I wanted to do what I did after the car accident. I wanted to sequester myself at home again. To unplug the phone and let the mail pile up. To build towers out of greasy take-out boxes.

But what would Anita have to say about that? She would tell me to pick up a cookbook and stop ordering take-out, for one. She would remind me that I was not alone—that there were people out there who, for one reason or another, were determined to be a part of my life. And that I should let them help me—because there are things you can do with help that you just can't do without.

I thought then that I might go to lunch with Julio and Rodolfo—maybe to that nice Peruvian restaurant.

We would start with an order of *ceviche*, and as Julio and Rodolfo argued over who was going to win that night's soccer match, I would notice a woman eating alone at the table next to ours. She would be engrossed in a thick book, and I would look down at her hands. They would be cracked and dirty.

"Don't look at my hands," she would say.

I would look up, startled.

"I'm embarrassed," she would say. "They're like that from working in the garden."

I would twist my chair around to face her. "You have a garden?"

"Oh yes," she would say. "Vegetables mostly, but I also have a few fruit trees—apricot and pear."

We would chat for a few moments. Her name would be Clara, and she would be a teacher. She would pay her bill and then reach over and give me a piece of paper with her phone number. I would call her the very next day. I would play it clean—no Manipulations, no "giving her a good day," no making her wait in my waiting room.

"So?" Rodolfo said. "Lunch?"

"I wouldn't say no to that Peruvian place," I said.

Julio thumped the steering wheel. "Consider it done!"

# EPILOGUE

I leaked the story of torture and child abuse at the Colony to several prominent newspapers upon my return to Santiago. Not a single one had the courage to publish a story that might result in repercussions from General Pinochet. Once General Pinochet stepped down from power, however—after a referendum in 1989—the media and the government were no longer forced to turn a blind eye towards Uncle Peter and the Colony.

The police began investigating a series of allegations that had emerged from a number of sources over the years, and I went to the police station and gave several hours of video-taped testimony. A warrant was issued by a prominent judge in Santiago, seeking to arrest Uncle Peter on charges of torture and child abuse. One morning, a team of police officers stormed through the gates. They searched high and low for Uncle Peter, but he was nowhere to be found. The interrogation room was discovered, and the few men who had made it out alive testified about the heinous acts of violence that had occurred there. The police continued to raid the Colony—more than thirty times over the next several years, but they could never find Uncle Peter.

Then, two major events sent everything into a tumble. The first occurred in March of 2005. A Chilean reporter had diligently interviewed dozens of colonists until she found some who were willing to cooperate—and one had told her that Uncle Peter made frequent trips to Argentina. The reporter followed a trail of evidence that led her to a small home in an exclusive gated community not far from Buenos Aires. She contacted the local authorities, who immediately sent a SWAT team. They swarmed the house and found Uncle Peter lying on a bed in the smallest room in the house. He looked drawn and sickly. Shortly after his arrest, he was extradited to Chile, where he was convicted of child molestation and a series of other charges ranging from tax evasion to murder. He was 86 years old.

Shortly thereafter, in 2006, only months after Uncle Peter's sentencing, General Pinochet suffered a heart attack (not his first) and subsequently died of congestive heart failure and pulmonary edema. He had narrowly avoided being convicted of a slew of charges on numerous occasions, and the country issued a collective sigh of relief when newspaper headlines proclaimed his death.

As for me, I met my Clara. Her name wasn't Clara—it was Lucía—and we didn't meet while eating lunch at the Peruvian restaurant but during the intermission of a play. We were in line for refreshments, and I struck up a conversation. Two of my students were in the play, I said, hoping to impress her. It turned out Lucía was the playwright. The lights flickered on and off, and we returned to our seats. I found her after the curtain call and invited her over for tea the next day to continue our conversation. We had carrot muffins—the carrots I had grown in my small backyard. With raisins.

Last week, Lucía went up north for a week to visit an ailing aunt, and I took the opportunity to visit the Colony—not that it was a Colony anymore, but simply a small town. I drove down the winding road, past the spot where Julio and Rodolfo had waited for me. I could see that the fence around the Colony had been torn down, but, otherwise, much of it seemed to be just as I had remembered it. I walked over to where the dining hall had been—a sign above the door read "La Cocina de Anita." I stepped inside the busy restaurant and a familiar-looking young woman offered to seat me. I studied her face carefully.

"Maca?" I said, finally.

She looked around. "How do you know my name?"

"It's me—Javier. You directed my play."

Maca's face lit up. She gave me a hug and held me at arm's length to look at me. Then there was an exclamation from the kitchen, and Anita came hurrying out.

"I was sure I'd never see you again," she said, hugging me. "Look at you."

She walked me over to a table by the window. "Now, you have a seat, and I'm going to make you something special," she said. Maca brought over a pair of menus.

"No menus," Anita said.

Maca returned a few minutes later. She brought with her a pitcher of water and a basket of warm, crusty bread. I filled myself up on bread but still found room to put away a green salad, a bowl of spicy seafood chowder, and a hefty slice of apple strudel.

"I have to ask," I said to Maca when she came to clear our plates, "did the colonists like the play?"

Maca put her stack of plates down on the table. She put a hand on her hip—and, for an instant, I could picture her in that exact same posture, as a child.

"They didn't get all of it," she said, finally. "I'm not sure I did, either. But they gave us a standing ovation. Everyone was so excited. They were all looking for you, but you were gone."

Anita came by to ask me if the food was to my liking. I reassured her that I would be returning to her restaurant as soon as I could. By this point, I was the only patron left, and I invited Anita and Maca to sit with me.

"What happened after I left?" I asked Anita.

"Uncle Peter told us that you and the goat man had been expelled from the Colony—that he had personally driven you to the seediest, darkest corner of Santiago and pushed you out of the car."

I told Anita and Maca what had really happened. In turn, they told me about how things had changed at the Colony after I left. There was a heightened sense of fear and anxiety after General Pinochet was voted out of power. Uncle Peter was away more and more often, and he appointed a Council of Elders to help him run the Colony. Then, one day, he was simply gone. No good-bye, no announcements from the Council of Elders—he was just there one day and gone the next. The Council refused to comment on his absence and tried to maintain the same iron grip that Uncle Peter had, but it was no use.

"We were not as afraid of them as we were of him," Maca said.

Their power continued to dwindle as the police raided the Colony more and more frequently. Shortly after Uncle Peter died, the Council of Elders disbanded, and the police tore down the fence that surrounded the Colony. Many Colonists fled instantly—others decided to stick around and try to create a serviceable town.

"The fields were all laid out, after all," Anita said. "The buildings were built, and the fruit trees were mature. There was no reason to walk away from all the hard work that had gone into this place."

With some help from the Chilean government, the Colony became incorporated as a town. They thought long and hard as to what to name it—finally, they decided on Río Pilón–the name of the river I had tumbled into as Santa Claus.

"They've brought in psychologists and doctors and social workers and God knows what else," Maca said. "To fix us. Anita and I are fine, but some of the others are not."

I nodded. I avoided asking about Ernesto—I was afraid of the answer I would get. The door to the restaurant swung open, and a young couple walked in. Maca excused herself, and Anita stood up.

"Come back soon, okay?" she said, hugging me tightly. I remembered the morning that I had cried in her arms.

"I've missed you," I said.

I left the restaurant and slowly walked down the street. I looked up and saw that the library had been painted a different colour and the sign altered to indicate that it was a public library, but the building was otherwise unchanged. I went inside, and a young man came eagerly around to the front of his desk to shake our hands.

"You must be new to town," he said. "Or you're visiting?"

"I'm looking for Ernesto," I said.

The young man looked down. "Ernesto's the one who taught me how to be a librarian," he said. "Ever since I was a little boy, I remember coming into the library to listen to him tell us stories."

I was afraid to ask the young man anything, so I let him continue.

"When I was old enough," he said, "Ernesto brought me in to learn how to be a librarian."

"You're the librarian now."

"I'm sorry," said the young man. "Ernesto passed away last year."

A part of me folded up into smaller and smaller squares, until it was gone.

"If you'd like to visit his grave," the young man said, "it's in the cemetery."

I nodded. I didn't trust myself to speak any more—not for some time. I began walking. The dirt road became grass, and I made my way up the gentle slopes of the cemetery. My feet remembered their way to Angela's grave. It was a little more overgrown but otherwise the same as it was the day Ernesto and I had walked here.

I read the inscription on it: "Our ship . . . " I thought of them boarding a ship in Seville. The grave beside Angela's—the one that was empty last time I was here—was now filled. It read, "Ernesto Cardozo 1910–2004."

And then, below that: ". . . has sailed."